A Dog About Town

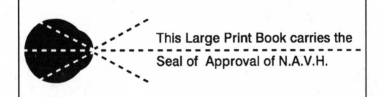

This Large Print Book carries the
Seal of Approval of N.A.V.H.

A DOG ABOUT TOWN

J. F. ENGLERT

THORNDIKE PRESS

An imprint of Thomson Gale, a part of The Thomson Corporation

THOMSON
GALE

Detroit • New York • San Francisco • New Haven, Conn. • Waterville, Maine • London

THOMSON

™

GALE

LIBRARY OF CONGRESS CATALOGING-IN-PUBLICATION DATA

Englert, J. F.
    A dog about town / by J.F. Englert.
        p. cm. — (Thorndike Press large print mystery)
        "A Bull Moose Dog Run mystery" — T.p. verso.
    ISBN-13: 978-0-7862-9824-2 (alk. paper)
    ISBN-10: 0-7862-9824-3 (alk. paper)
    1. Labrador retriever — Fiction. 2. Dogs — Fiction. 3. Human-animal relationships — Fiction. 4. Murder — Fiction. 5. Occultists — Fiction. 6. Manhattan (New York, N.Y.) — Fiction. 7. Large type books. I. Title.
PS3605.N48D64 2007
813'.6—dc22   2007022067

Published in 2007 by arrangement with The Bantam Dell Publishing Group, a division of Random House, Inc.

Printed in the United States of America on permanent paper
10 9 8 7 6 5 4 3 2 1

For Penelope

ACKNOWLEDGMENTS

I would like to thank Danielle Perez for her fine editorial counsel; Dan Craig for the superb portrait of Randolph in his smoking jacket; Patricia Ballantyne and everyone at Bantam Dell for their work; Micahlyn Whitt; Steve Malko; Matthew Sweeney; Peter Thomas; Susan Stava for her photography; and Claudia Cross at Sterling Lord Literistic for making sure that Randolph found a good home.

Dogs are wise. They crawl away into a quiet corner and lick their wounds and do not rejoin the world until they are whole once more.

— Agatha Christie

A Body in the Bathroom
A Number 1 in Central Park

Lyell Overton Minskoff-Hardy, literary light and cultural personage, perished a few days before Christmas beneath a stainless steel toilet on the Upper West Side of Manhattan. With his fly open. Harry, my owner, prone to accept all explanations involving the paranormal, believed the death had a supernatural flourish. Almost from the start I thought Harry quite mistaken. Overton's death had nothing to do with ghosts, spirits or the occult and everything to do with science, human nastiness and greed.

I first learned of Overton's death upon the return of my owner to our humble walk-up apartment. I had been rereading Robert Pinsky's excellent translation *The Inferno of Dante,* an artifact from Imogen's time in our lives, when I heard the familiar clump-clump on the stairs and the jangle and click of locks being opened — notably more urgent than usual. I did not have time to close the book or even move too far away from it. I imagined my owner's imminent surprise. The book would be the first thing he would notice, no doubt. The reading light that had been off when he departed would be the second.

I was wrong. Harry was in such a distracted state that he noticed nothing out of the ordinary. Rain dripped from his Driza-Bone jacket and pooled on the kitchen floor. My owner is a broad-shouldered, strapping fellow, standing almost six foot three, and you would never guess that his regular regimen of physical fitness had long been derailed by frequent retreats to the La-Z-Boy recliner with buckets of fried chicken and takeout Chinese.

"A great man is dead tonight, Randolph," he pronounced.

I could think of several great men who were dead that night. Dante Alighieri, Florentine poet, first among them; Sir Winston Churchill, a close second, but I did not so much as growl a qualifier.

"A famous man," Harry emphasized.

He crammed what looked like a Maryland crab cake into our deeply troubled refrigerator, the interior of which had remained a shadowland of petrified broccoli and pizza since the bulb burned out months before.

"Lyell Overton Minskoff-Hardy." Harry spoke the dead man's name with a kind of reverence.

It is a point of pride that I remain well acquainted with the biographies of luminaries past and present. I do this chiefly through newspapers and magazines. There is much truth to be gleaned from the gossip columns. Rich treasures of it. I had already assembled a full mental file of notes on the man Harry named and I drew from it now.

Lyell Overton Minskoff-Hardy was two men really. There was the patrician figure, Lyell Overton, whose name evoked English estates and private libraries where wolfhounds stretch before the sputtering hearth and leather-bound volumes lie open awaiting the return of some tousle-haired savant from Oxford. An appropriate image, I think, for he was tall and graceful in that insouciant, underclassman way — a perennial student and college man, his torso forever sheathed in the invisible, but palpable, entitlement of the varsity letter sweater.

The Minskoff-Hardy contribution was gritty, ethnic and glamorous in a hard-won sort of way. It was Broadway via Ellis Island and the Five Points — vintage New York. Minskoff-Hardy could be urbane and worldwise, but also, as are so many native New

13

Yorkers, hopelessly parochial, predisposed to view with suspicion anything not found or imported to their narrow island. Minskoff-Hardy was brash and full of colic, demanding and impatient. But more than anything, Minskoff-Hardy was ambitious and his ambition had wounded, scarred and made an army of permanent enemies along the way.

Both men inhabiting the hyphenated identity died that night with their flys open, their eyelids slightly ajar and their last bon mot left unspoken.

These matters of temper and temperament are now locked in his dead heart, but his death — and this moment with Harry in our cramped but cozy Upper West Side abode — would bring out that inner being in Yours Truly concerned with the murderous significance of details and the disastrous consequences that stem from small gestures. All such questions of the heart and the character are my concern because the detective is the last true humanist, standing at that lonely intersection where observation and reason meet emotion and intuition revealing the secrets that measure our fragile, inconstant, but extraordinary beings. How ironic, then, that I am not even human.

Yes, that is correct. I am *not* human.

You see, I am a dog — not a scoundrel, a cad, a rascal — no, not a dog in that sense, but an actual dog, *Canis familiaris.* One of the most familiar and lovable (I only repeat the general perception): a Labrador retriever. A Labrador retriever is defined by Merriam-Webster as "any of a breed of compact, strongly built retrievers largely developed in England from stock originating in Newfoundland and having a short dense black, yellow, or chocolate coat . . . called also *Lab, Labrador.*" Faithful to that definition, I am indeed compact and strongly built (though bulging at the midsection from my owner's generous feedings) and black but for a wisp of premature white on my chin that serves to impart a sort of sage-like impression.

I am also sentient. I can think. I can remember. I can understand that as the teller of this tale I had best get most of this explanatory material over with at the beginning. Like the reader, I compare the past and the present. I strategize and calculate. This is not a possibility entertained by the Merriam-Webster definition. The competent editors of that publication are not to blame for the oversight. Most dogs certainly do not behave in ways that would suggest

15

sentience (though I might also add that most humans do not either as is apparent from the hastiest of glances at the newspapers). Moreover, there is at present no way to penetrate my species' muteness. Science is unable to plumb the depths of our cerebral cortices and discern the life of our minds.

Even so, among my brothers and sisters, I am unique. Where other dogs babble, I sing. Where they follow tangents like they are darting from scent to scent, my thoughts are precision-guided. If you could speak our language, you would understand. It is a challenge to extract a single relevant word from one of my brethren let alone a competent sentence and forget reasonable analysis altogether. It's all myth, rumor and constant distraction with them. What makes my kind endearing to humans makes them difficult for me to endure. It is a mystery why I am different. Genetic mutation, something in the water my mother drank during her pregnancy, my rearing, who knows? I came to consciousness, I suspect, in much the same way a human child does: sticky scraps of reality gradually collaged into a bigger picture within which an identity was assumed.

"Randolph, tonight was unbelievable,"

Harry said finally. "It's going to be all over the papers tomorrow."

He forced the refrigerator closed with a grunt. I had the momentary sense that something might try to escape.

"One minute Overton was at the table telling stories: a taxi ride with Truman Capote; strip poker with Kerouac; arm wrestling with Fidel Castro . . ."

Harry reached behind the toaster for his emergency cigarettes. He shook one free from the pack, lit it and put the rest into his pocket.

"Halfway through dinner, Overton gets up, walks down the hall, then there's a sort of yelp. I expected that he would burst out into the dining room with a joke; instead he was dying on the bathroom floor in a pool of urine. A woman found him. I think she owned the apartment. At least, she acted like she did, but I don't think she is the one who invited me."

Harry had been invited to assist at a séance that night. The invitation had come through the mail with no return address. Harry wasn't too sure who had invited him, but he accepted anyway — lately he had become vulnerable to the promises of the paranormal and immersed himself in that otherworldly network of charlatans and misty-eyed believers. It was a fascination that was trying my patience even though I understood the tragedy that had caused it — a tragedy that had crippled me as well and made it impossible to act with any decisiveness for many months.

"She acted like she owned Overton too, because she kept nagging him. When she found him, she screamed. We didn't even get to the real part of the séance. Overton wanted us to contact his first wife. She had died on their wedding night. He said she was his true love . . ."

Harry's voice trailed off, leaving only the hollow, tinny sound of rainwater down our drainpipe and his crisp inhale. I knew he was thinking of Imogen; talk of true love always had this effect on him. Imogen was *our* tragedy.

Less than a year earlier Imogen had left our apartment for an evening walk. She was going to Zabar's to buy some bread. She often made this trip on the nights she returned home early from her work as an archivist at the Morgan Library — that fabulous New York institution endowed long ago by the solitaire-playing tycoon J. P. Morgan. Imogen liked to buy bread at the end of the day. It was usually marked down, but more than this, the idea of getting bread daily appealed to her romantic nature. She told Harry that it made her feel like we were living in Paris and she had ducked down to the *boulangerie* for a baguette.

But that night she didn't return. Harry launched a massive search. He enlisted the police. He rallied friends. He chased down every lead he received and spent hours in excruciating vigil by the phone. Weeks passed. The police finally found her red beret under a bench in Riverside Park. The assumption was that she had somehow fallen into the water and drowned. At least that was one assumption, but darker visions of my mistress's fate haunted me. Her body was not found and she remained a missing person.

Harry and I had been living a sort of half-life of false starts and impossible expectations ever since in the same apartment to which we three had all moved so happily, filled with future promise. Harry and Imogen had met at a party downtown — a party that she frequently liked to remind him she had almost skipped because her Labrador puppy had a cold that night.

Harry took another long, reflective drag of his cigarette. I tried to keep my body motionless but the involuntary canine trembling that many humans mistake for excitement made my collar tinkle.

Harry mistook the sound for bladder-based urgency. He took my leash down from the hook beside the door and clapped his big hands together.

"Want to go for a walk, boy?"

Harry employed the singsong voice reserved for inducing the delivery of a swift Number 1 or 2 by Yours Truly.

I sat down and let him snap the leash to my collar. I am fortunate in this important regard: he is sensitive to my need for walks, seldom inflicting a marathon of waiting that might force me to test my house-trained credentials.

It was well past midnight and our street was empty. It had stopped raining, but the sidewalk still glistened. Young Harry remained silent. He sucked the life out of his cigarette and lit a second. Together we exhaled great clouds of steam and smoke into the cold night air as we trotted toward Central Park. We crossed the avenue, passed through the park gate and down the tree-lined path. The ground was hard beneath my paws, but a little spongy in places from the rain. Indeed, it felt like December — winter but not quite.

My nose filled with an inexplicably rich array of winter smells. Smells are a central fact of my universe. I will do my best to share them with you despite the extreme differences in our noses which, to make a wine-tasting parallel, will reduce the finest vintage for you to a third-rate beer for me. What a marvelous organ! A Labrador's sense of smell is 100,000 times more acute than that of man. Imagine what the world would be like if humans could smell with the same complexity. Humans would have at their disposal a rich vocabulary that could illuminate nuance and shed truth. But more on that later.

Even in the absence of need, I never forget to pull Harry toward the little hill that has been designated for my Number 1s. I think if I act a bit Pavlovian it reinforces the importance of regular walks in my owner's mind. That night, I lifted my right leg and as usual felt embarrassed even though there was no one else about.

Not that Harry was paying me the slightest bit of attention. He was off with the pixies — sad and brokenhearted pixies.

"Sometimes," Harry said, "the spirits will call to us so strongly that our bodies just let us go. Maybe that's what happened to Overton. Maybe his first wife was calling from the beyond."

Malarkey, of course, but I couldn't blame

Harry. Imogen had left us both quite alone, forced to pick up the fragments as best we could and lick wounds that showed no sign of healing. Harry had responded to her absence by opening himself up to people and ideas that Imogen would have promptly dismissed as fools and absurdities — and Harry would have felt the same confident disdain in happier times.

If Imogen's disappearance had taught me anything it was this: men need to be loved or they will slowly and invariably go bad. A perfectly adequate male in his twenties will become, in little more than a decade — if unloved — a strange creature statistically prone to die of an ingrown toenail in an apartment crammed with hoarded newspapers and unwashed cereal bowls.

Harry wasn't the only male that could use Imogen's help. I was also slipping without her. She had been my mistress long before she had been Harry's. My mind scrolled backward five years.

"Aren't you a wise little dog?" Imogen had said, lifting my puppy body high in the air and gently flicking my chin, white even then. That very day she had whisked me away from the pet store clods, the sawdust and the poking children to my first home: a little studio in the East Village.

Imogen had made better males of us both and yet the anatomy of my dog's eyes would never permit me to shed a single tear for my vanished mistress.

A Dog Reviews a Journal
A Strange Code is Discovered

As Harry and I trudged up the stairs from our walk, it suddenly occurred to me that I had encountered Overton's name before and much closer to home than the tabloid gossip pages. The dead auteur was mentioned in Imogen's journal. My mistress was fun-loving and at times even a little bit wild, but she had — as befitted her profession — an archivist's thoroughness and this was especially apparent in the regularity and precision of her journal entries. She had kept a journal since high school, but I only had access to the final volume — a thin marbleized notebook that remained faceup on the lowest shelf of the bookcase (the rest were tucked away in a cardboard box in the bedroom closet). This notebook contained scores of entries penned in black ink and Imogen's fine, precise hand.

Harry peeled off his rain gear and made his way to the La-Z-Boy. I curled up, wet and matted, beside the bookcase. When my owner was firmly engrossed in the *New York Post* and exhaling massive plumes of cigarette smoke, I carefully nosed the journal onto the floor, opened it and began to leaf through. In the months after Imogen's disappearance, I had spent a great deal of time poring over this volume. I had heard in the firm but delicate prose the silent echo of my mistress's voice. For a while, I had even hoped that somehow some direction, some hint of what to do and how to find her might be hidden in the entries, but there was usually little more than musings on what she had for lunch, a newly noticed quirk about Harry or a particularly stunning sunset seen on the way home.

But now I was searching for a specific: Overton. I knew that he was somewhere in these pages and I found him in the concluding paragraphs of the last entry — the entry Imogen made the night before she disappeared:

Lyell Overton came to the archives today. I have never met him in person before but he has called us a few times. He is a striking man on television — I've seen him interviewed on *Charlie Rose* — but in person there is something small about him even though he isn't physically small at all. There is something almost mean about him. I know that's not nice and might not be true, but there it is. Anyway, he told me — and this was a surprise — that he was going to write a book that would define his career. "*The* book," he said. It was to be nonfiction and incredibly researched. It would do for him (he almost shouted this part) what *In Cold Blood* had done for Truman Capote. He didn't say what the book was about exactly, but he suggested that part of its importance rested in a family saga. "And that, my young and considerably attractive lady, is where I require your expertise." I am not joking. Overton actually said that to me. And then he said something weird, something a little spooky . . . Gotta go . . . It's Harry's turn to cook so that means we're having takeout — ha! . . . More later . . .

The entry ended there, followed by dozens of empty pages . . . Or what I had always assumed were empty pages, because now as I idly turned a few I saw that this entry wasn't, in fact, the last. Imogen had uncharacteristically abandoned order and under the date of her disappearance on a random page, had written:

Overton at the archives again. Disturbing
. . . He says he fears for his life . . . And
there are other things too . . .

The entry was followed after an inch of
white space by a curious string of letters
and numbers:

$$_{12}CDYZMNBCEFLMIJNOEF8_9$$

If my long, white-bearded chin could have
dropped and hit the floor, it would have
done so with a profound bang. I had a stunning revelation before me. One that changed
everything. The inertia, the pain, the futile
dead space after her disappearance . . . but
now there was a reason, something to hold
on to, even the possibility of someone still
out there to retrieve . . .
In the brief period between Imogen's
return from work and her departure for the
errand from which she never returned, she
had revealed in the pages of her journal that
something was seriously wrong that day.
Overton had been afraid of foul play (and
he was now dead). *And there are other things
too . . .*
And these revelations were followed by a
code.

Ghost Hunting in New Jersey
A Dog's Curiosity
is Further Aroused

The intercom buzzed without end indicating that some early riser was seeking entrance downstairs.

Neither Harry nor I had slept much the night before. After hours of vainly attempting to make 12CDYZMNBCEFLMIJNOEF8₉ reveal its secret, I had managed a few fitful hours between dreams of a blueblood writer — the best version of a grainy tabloid image of Lyell Overton Minskoff-Hardy my mind could produce. He was lying on a bathroom floor sobbing like an infant. He sobbed and sobbed and then turned to look at me with a face that had suddenly become Imogen's. In the early morning hours I puzzled over the dream and the code again but to no avail. I lay supine in my corner — the designated spot in the apartment for most of my naps and loungings. I looked up at the easels, curled canvases and Harry's unfinished painting of Imogen with her dark honey hair spilling down — the last work among a series now seemingly destined to remain incomplete.

I heard Harry awake in the bedroom. I don't know why exactly, but I had not slept there since Imogen had disappeared. My owner uttered an expletive and jumped to his feet as the buzzer transitioned into "Shave and a Haircut, Two Bits."

The culprit was Ivan Manners, who had arrived on time with Mr. Apples for a previously scheduled appointment. Ivan is a self-styled ghost hunter and expert on the paranormal. Harry had met him during those vulnerable months after Imogen's disappearance when my owner turned to the other world for the answers he could not find in this one. As a result of the meeting, Harry came to serve as Ivan's sometimes apprentice on fruitless expeditions to catch some evidence of the supernatural with the flypaper of technology. Mr. Apples is a rainbow lorikeet who speaks Farsi because his first owner was an Iranian taxi driver.

Harry stumbled over the Pinsky translation as he made his way to the front door and kicked it deep into the wilderness beneath the daybed.

"We'll be right down," Harry shouted into the intercom.

Ivan is stout, loud and self-consciously eccentric. His real name is Allen Stewart Manners but he insists that everyone address him as Ivan because its harsh Slavic sound mirrors the no-nonsense spiritual Cossack that he imagines himself to be. He is of independent means — fueled by a seemingly inexhaustible trust fund — and spent his twenties in a half dozen different graduate programs from which he never exited with a degree. Ivan believes that he has psychic powers that aid in his work as a paranormal investigator. I have never seen any evidence of this supposed gift, but he managed to get this ability and his ghost hunting showcased on daytime TV and his phone has been ringing off the hook ever since.

This time a distraught housewife had contacted Ivan. She believed that her family was living with a poltergeist. The plan was to cram everyone including Yours Truly into Ivan's lavender Mini Cooper for the trip to Paramus, New Jersey. In addition to us, the tiny vehicle was to be filled with electromagnetic field detectors (EMFs), cameras for capturing spectral orbs and tape recorders for supernatural groans, sighs and whispers.

Harry pulled on jeans and a sweater. Once he was dressed, I produced a short whine lest my breakfast be overlooked in our headlong rush out the door. Ivan and Mr. Apples would be near intolerable on an empty stomach. Before I had to use more drastic measures, my owner reached into the refrigerator and rescued the crab cake from the night before. He tossed it into my bowl and I ate with gusto, brushing my snout against the crab fragments for maximum olfactory benefit.

When we reached the street to find Ivan's Mini Cooper idling at the curb, my owner stepped over a discarded newspaper in our path. It was that day's *New York Post.* The double-barreled headline blared:

AUTHOR TOILET TRAGEDY — TO PEE OR NOT TO PEE

We crossed the George Washington Bridge and sped down Route 4. I wedged my nose into the rush of oncoming air. New Jersey smelled as unpromising as usual. Usually the intensity of smells is as heady as a drug (uncouth dogs have described it to me as window speedball), but today I got a lungful of diesel exhaust from a caravan of tractor-trailers and SUVs before pulling myself back into the car.

Ivan mauled his second donut. Mr. Apples

muttered unintelligibly and struggled for a foothold on the backseat beside me. Harry related Overton's death as Ivan squinted for the exit to Paramus. The ghost-hunting psychic appeared utterly uninterested in the literary giant's expiration.

"He was overrated. And old. And his books were boring," Ivan said. "And he'd already had a bloody heart attack."

"Really, a heart attack?" Harry asked. "When?"

"I read about it a few years ago. Actually, it wasn't a heart attack. They just put in a bloody pacemaker. Why they wasted the news space for it, I don't know. Stuff like that makes me nuts. Who cares? He's just one guy who had a lousy everyday operation. The media's worthless."

Ivan bit a chunk out of his third donut.

"Bloody worthless."

Ivan was fond of the word *bloody* and hoped to pioneer its introduction into American English.

Ten minutes later, we pulled up in front of an enormous house with a green mailbox and a giant plastic snowman deflating on the front lawn. The house was one of those excessive structures built in the nineties, a particleboard mansion that swallowed an entire family in echoing caverns of faux luxury with an oval above the door large enough to hold the window of the cathedral at Chartres.

Even though I anticipated Harry's initial paranormal assessment of the situation, I still winced when it came out of the mouth of the grown man who was responsible for feeding, housing and walking me.

"Indian burial ground," Harry said. "Too new a house for anything else. You agree?"

"Bloody good possibility — but be careful about jumping to conclusions, especially when it comes to structural newness. I found an apparition living in a three-month-old condo in Hoboken. Sometimes recent construction is just as good as old for a portal to the other world."

Before Ivan had a chance to ring the bell a woman opened the door. She looked embattled and straddled a blond-topped toddler on her hip.

"We think it's in the laundry room," the woman said.

She eyed the two ghost hunters' animal companions.

"Leave the dog and the parrot in the car."

"Mr. Apples is not a parrot. He is a rainbow lorikeet." Ivan said.

"Never mind. They can come too."

The woman waved all four of us into the

interior.

Ivan bustled past her. Two tape recorders, a digital video camera, a red-beamed flash-light, an EMF and a crackling walkie-talkie dangled from his body.

"We'll take general readings first," Ivan said. "Be free, Mr. Apples."

The bird began to swoop about the enor-mous living room, menacing table lamps and colliding with the ceiling fan.

"Does he have to do that?" the woman asked. "I just had it painted."

"Birds live close to the spirit world," Ivan said. "If something is happening, Mr. Apples will know about it."

Mr. Apples settled on a ledge twenty feet above us and began picking at a dead spider.

"Follow me," Ivan said.

The laundry room was bare except for a calendar of the farmhouses of Vermont and a bulk-sized box of powdered detergent next to an enormous carton of *Berrylicious* juice boxes.

"What exactly happens here?" Ivan asked the woman.

"Besides washing?"

Ivan waved his hand dismissively. "Of course."

"Noises mostly. Things get knocked over. The machines run by themselves. You're not as handsome in person as you were on TV."

Ivan stuck his head in the dryer.

"Your friend's very handsome, but he wasn't on TV."

The woman stared at Harry admiringly. My owner blushed.

"What kind of noises?" Ivan asked.

"A clearing-your-throat kind of sound. Once there was a sneeze."

"I'm getting a higher reading near the dryer," Ivan said. "Did you buy the dryer new or used?"

"New."

"Are you sure?" Ivan asked. "It could be a portable haunting. Objects can carry strong psychic payloads. Wherever they end up that's where the haunting occurs. I had a toaster in Queens put out 9.4 EMFs. The cord had been used in a suicide."

"New. We definitely bought it new."

"Interesting."

Ivan ducked behind the machine.

"Temperature is dropping," Harry said.

"How much?"

"Two degrees since we left the hallway."

"Very interesting," Ivan said.

I noted that the unfinished floors and walls of the laundry room were the most likely source of the drop in temperature. This obvious fact was lost on my two ghost hunters. Ivan pursued the dryer angle.

"Has it been repaired?"

"As a matter of fact, it has."

"Do you know if any parts were changed?"

Ivan pulled the unit away from the wall and began filming the back of the dryer.

The woman thought for a minute.

"The repairman said something about a belt."

"That's a bloody part."

Ivan's expression was now quite smug.

"I suggest that you take the child to a secure area," the ghost hunter instructed the woman. "We've found your problem."

"Harry, shut off the lights. I'm going nite-vision."

Having accompanied the pair on more than a few of these pointless exercises, I was aware that Ivan favored filming using the infrared feature on his store-bought video camera. The images that resulted were green, granular and distorted. Under such visual conditions a pan-fried dumpling would resemble a spectral presence.

A Labrador requires twelve hours of sleep a day and the mental and physical exhaustion of the hours since Harry returned with news of Overton's death and the revelations in Imogen's journal suddenly overwhelmed me. I found a reasonably cozy corner for a nap. After fifteen minutes or so, during which I was vaguely aware of Ivan and Harry interviewing something they referred to as "the entity," the session had concluded.

"I have negotiated a truce," Ivan said as we exited the laundry room and encountered the lady of the house whose name was Belinda.

"A truce?"

"If you limit your use of the dryer to the high/cotton setting, the entity will remain at peace."

"What about my lingerie?"

"Air-dry."

"You can't be serious."

Ivan shrugged.

"This is the agreement with the entity. If you wish to violate it for the sake of a brassiere that is your prerogative, but I can't be held responsible for the consequences."

"How did this thing get into my house?"

"The replacement belt," Ivan said. "If you inquire, you will find that the belt is not a new part, but reconditioned and involved in some indeterminate but tragic incident. The entity mentioned something about a lawn mower and a nude sunbather."

The blond child pulled at Belinda's pant leg.

"What do I owe you?" she asked Ivan.

"Not a cent. Your case has helped advance the study of the paranormal. However, a modest donation to the Lorikeet Rescue Fund would be appreciated. Remember: *a bird without seed is a bird in need.*"

Ivan patted down his body to make sure that no equipment had been left behind.

"Now for Mr. Apples," Ivan announced.

He held up his arm and Mr. Apples dropped from his perch where in short order the bird had soiled all of the neighboring walls.

Harry was well out the door when Belinda addressed him.

"Are you involved?"

"Involved?"

"Do you date?"

"No."

"Never?"

"Nope."

"Are you gay?"

"No."

"That's too bad."

"What's too bad?"

"About the not dating, not about the not being gay."

"Why?"

"You know what I mean," Belinda said. "It's not for me if that's what you're thinking, but I've got someone who would be perfect for you. She's about your age, she's beautiful, she eats organic and she's in the entertainment industry."

Harry turned and walked across the yellow lawn to the car.

"I'm taken," he said, stepping over the deflated snowman.

My owner patted his chest lightly. This gesture had become a reflex. On a thick silver chain beneath his sweater hung the engagement ring that he had bought but never given to Imogen.

"Your dog should really lose some weight," Belinda called after him. I was momentarily stung by the gratuity of the comment, but such nit-picking is a typical human response to not getting one's way. I had a few possible but inexpressible ripostes. She was, after all, what they call a dye job and the stick-figure opposite of my body's healthy abundance. Instead I chose the diplomatic route. Harry responded more than adequately.

"Randolph's fine just the way he is."

We all got into the Mini and Ivan squealed around the cul-de-sac and onto the main road, Belinda waving from the stoop.

I was happy to be going home. I am a city dog and find the suburbs' sprawl unnerving. The city has its distinct neighborhoods and its small sanctuaries, its way of being and its logic. Whenever I have left my island home, I have felt a strange constriction in my throat and the stray palpitation of my heart. The prosperous chaos of the suburbs bleeds out into the chaos of America, bleeds out into the plains, the mountains and finally that other ocean. Then America itself bleeds into the world and the world bleeds into the universe.

Manhattan has proven universe enough for me. Here, at least, I feel mostly at home. Within fifteen minutes we had reached the George Washington Bridge and had begun to cross back into the city. I looked out over that great electric hubbub that F. Scott Fitzgerald wrote had "all the iridescence of the beginning of the world," and found myself contemplating Overton again as the car and conversation faded into a meditative rumble.

I wondered whether the man, who could not help but wound through his ambition, had reflected upon unrealized literary achievement in his last conscious moment. Or had he simply frozen in disbelief at the approaching prospect of personal extinction over a toilet bowl. He was, after all, a man who was "crowned before [he] was king" as the composer Mascagni once said of himself on his early glory and his future lack of achievement. Overton's first book, written when he was barely nineteen, was an immediate sensation. Everything else that followed was a failed, though best-selling, reprisal and transparent imitation of that initial success.

His reputation in the writing life had been launched and sustained by this pedigree of mid-twentieth-century entitlement and superiority, which by the time of his death in the twenty-first century was anachronistic. Nevertheless, the pedigree lent his books, his commentary (there were volumes), his literary journal (of which he was cofounder and longtime editor) and his public conversation, a mixture of gravitas and exuberance that was like champagne served in a leaden flute, a beverage of bubbles framed by the certain knowledge of a broken and ancient world. But still in that eternal solitary artist's garret to which all writers come at last to be judged, Overton must have suspected that he would finally be found a failure.

Imogen's journal entry suggested this at least — a sense of struggling against the inevitability of such judgment by seeking to create one last, career-redeeming work. And then, of course, there was Imogen's secret and the strange characters $12CDYZMNBCE-FLMIJNOEF8_9$. My brain had reached a dead end for the moment, but as Sherlock Holmes proclaimed in *The Adventure of the Dancing Men* and I now echoed silently to myself: *These hieroglyphics have evidently a meaning. If it is a purely arbitrary one, it may be impossible for us to solve it. If, on the other hand, it is systematic, I have no doubt that we shall get to the bottom of it.* Imogen and Overton were connected somehow and these characters — if they were "systematic" — might hold the answer.

We reached the Manhattan side of the river and the car veered onto the off-ramp.

"Why couldn't you just tell her to change the belt?" Harry asked Ivan.

Bravo, I thought, finally the boy was using his gray matter.

"There are risks," Ivan said in the studied tone of the professional pseudoscientist who must justify his line of work with jargon. "Spectral product jumping is only the most obvious. By now, you see, the entity might be content to remain in the dryer, even if the belt is replaced."

Harry nodded, buying it hook, line and bloody sinker. *Ridiculous,* I huffed (my huff came out like a half bark that earned a distracted pat from my owner and a fumbled treat). The study of the paranormal casts a numbing spell on reason. Hadn't Watson and Cloftfeather's fine study, *Charlatans and Wishful Thinking; The (Para) psychology of the Occult,* dismissed the kind of nonsense that regularly came from Ivan's lips? I couldn't wait to get to our little apartment.

I had begun to drowse when Overton's name was mentioned again. Harry, it seemed, could not accept how such a vibrant man might simply perish.

"It was like turning off a switch," Harry said.

Ivan had relaxed after the ghost hunt and seemed more inclined to entertain the story of Overton's final moments.

"That's death for some, Harry. Sudden and shocking. The death that the dead didn't even see coming. That kind of death keeps me very busy." Ivan yawned.

"Half the time the ghost doesn't even know it's dead," he said. "Overton's probably still babbling away at the dinner table and wondering why no one's laughing at his jokes. A few weeks from now the fine china will go flying against the wall and my services will be required."

"It was terrible watching him die," Harry said.

"Like I said, he was old. Now he's moved

on. We all have to move on. The terror of death is all smoke screen," Ivan said. "Wait a minute. You didn't actually watch him die, did you? Didn't you say that he was dead when you got to the bathroom?"

Harry furrowed his brow.

"Not exactly."

"You didn't see an ectoplasmic event, did you? Tell me you didn't see an ectoplasmic event. I'm going to cry foul bloody murder if you did and didn't have your bloody camera with you."

Ivan pushed the pedal of the Mini flush with the floor and the lavender ghost mobile sped down the inside lane of the Westside Highway in a brake-light-smearing fury.

"Not exactly," Harry said.

A black Lincoln Town Car swerved out of our lane in an effort to avoid a horrific collision and the turban of its Sikh driver slid to a forty-five-degree angle.

"Use your bloody blinker, you bloody moron," Ivan roared. "Not exactly? What exactly does 'not exactly' mean?"

"He was still alive when we reached the bathroom. He was talking."

"Talking?"

"Not talking precisely, but able to talk . . . a little," Harry said.

The lavender Mini screamed down the

Ninety-sixth Street exit ramp, around the switchback curve and onto Riverside Drive.

"He spoke one word."

"What word?" Ivan asked.

Elektra.

I could tell my owner was still upset by the memory.

"The man said Elektra," Harry repeated.

Ivan whistled.

"Elektra? He really said Elektra?"

"What's interesting about Elektra?" Harry asked.

"Nothing," Ivan said. "Just a whole bloody hell of a lot. Remember Sophocles' play of the same name?"

"I don't have a clue," my owner said, although he should have. Imogen had spent the better part of one Sunday morning gently educating her young man about ancient Greek drama among the tousled sheets, the coffee and the *New York Times.* Those were good days for our little family.

"Elektra, my friend, is the daughter who loves her father in a most undaughterly way — the female equivalent of Oedipus. Now in literature Elektra is one thing; in the spirit world she is that and something more, something deeply primal — a profound erotic connection between dead and living."

Ivan gunned his engine to encourage an

elderly woman with a walker to hasten across the intersection where we stood stopped at a red light.

"So Overton saying Elektra means something?" Harry asked.

"You're bloody damn right it does."

Ivan pushed the pedal down hard as the light changed and the Mini fishtailed up the hill.

"What does it mean?"

"Bloody hell if I know. I know it means something. Overton saying it suggests that some powerful spirit was there to bring him across. He was not alone. In short, it was a bloody ectoplasmic event. Did he say anything else?"

"No. That was all I heard. The owner of the apartment told us to leave the bathroom. Then the ambulance came."

Ivan double-parked outside the stoop of our building on West Ninetieth Street, a careworn brownstone whose ornate but tired façade hinted at the grand era before it had been broken up into a dozen one-bedroom apartments. Harry stepped out and I wedged half of my body down onto the pavement and waited for the rest to follow.

"Mark my words," said Ivan, "we haven't heard the last of Mr. Overton Minskoffwhat's-his-name."

For once Ivan was onto something.

Danger at the Bull Moose Dog Run
Something Important is Learned

It is not easy for a dog to watch his owner take a buffoon seriously, especially when that buffoon is the chronically domineering Ivan Manners. Harry lacked his old confidence. Deep, irreparable sadness sucked his strength and a desperate hope that somehow things might be put right — in this world or the next — made him tolerate behavior that he never would have accepted in earlier days. At times like this, I felt my own sadness diminish and a certain protective resolve grow in its place. *He needs you, Randolph,* I could almost hear Imogen say.

As soon as Ivan and Mr. Apples drove off into the evening, I pulled Harry in the direction of the Bull Moose Dog Run.

The Bull Moose Dog Run is an enclosed expanse of dirt and pebbles beside the American Museum of Natural History and in the shadow of the great glass box that is its Rose Center for Earth and Space. I am comforted and inspired by this edifice to the sheer empirical boldness of our continuing leap into the stars. One day, perhaps, I will somehow gain access to the extraordinary Hayden Planetarium housed in the giant metallic sphere at the center of the complex and return, if only in reenactment, to the first explosive moments of the universe.

Owners and their pets come to this dusty pen in great numbers throughout the day. Temporarily liberated from the leash law, a ragtag bunch of my kind — purebreds and mutts — scamper, sniff, chase and nip their way around the run.

The purpose for most canine outings in New York City is bodily necessity. You can tell a lot about a dog by the way he or she approaches a Number 1 and a Number 2. There are, for example, the *Zigzag Dumpers* for whom a Number 2 is impossible if not preceded by a pell-mell dash through the undergrowth with their owners either leashed in tow or shouting from a quarter mile away. Then there are the *Squat-and-Drops. Squat-and-Drops* never stand on ceremony. They couldn't care less who was in the immediate vicinity. When they need to do their business, there is no stopping them. A New York dog run has all kinds. Plenty of *Zigzag Dumpers* and *Squat-and-Drops,* of course, but also the more demure *Foliage-Finders,* who refuse to be seen in process; the picky *Asphalt-Onlys* (real city dogs), who never go on grass or dirt, and their opposites, the *Earth-Onlys,* who never go on the asphalt. It is tempting to be breedist, assume a bulldog will be a *Squat-and-Drop* and a poodle a *Foliage-Finder,* but this would be a mistake. I have known the best-groomed poodles to act like shameless *Squat-and-Drops* and more than one Alaskan husky has proven an easily embarrassed *Foliage-Finder* (more Yours Truly's speed).

The *Squat-and-Drops* were out in full force when Harry and I arrived at the dog run. The *Foliage-Finders* — by far the most amiable of personalities — were nowhere to be seen. A hyperactive greyhound raced between legs in an attempt to harass an Alsatian; an anorexic toy poodle fresh from the dog show circuit shivered in the chill night air beneath a custom-made cashmere sweater; and an army of Jack Russells chased a single tennis ball thrown by a man using a device that was a cross between a long-handled spade and a pasta tosser. I had seen the device before. It was in vogue on the Upper West Side and enabled owners to play fetch without getting their hands dirty or putting undue stress on the lumbar regions of their backs. Human beings are a strange breed indeed.

Harry, sans pasta tosser, has tried fetch with me on several occasions. I have never shown any interest. Though I sometimes feel stirrings to run, I don't want to try the game lest Harry get himself into the very bad habit of expecting me to fetch every time we go for a walk.

Owners, you see, fall into categories just as easily as their pets. There seem to be two major pet-owning characters: the *Apologizers* and the *Apologists.* The *Apologizers* take the blame for everything their dog does or does not do. They do so vocally and with body language, usually sweeping gestures of surprise and shrinking postures of shame. The *Apologizer* seems shocked that his or her dog would push through the legs of a crowd at the intersection or do a Number 2 right in the middle of the street. The *Apologist* is the exact opposite. He — it's usually a he — seems to take pride when his hundred-pound junkyard dog mounts someone's long-haired Chihuahua or gobbles down a child's ice cream. The *Apologist's* animal is like a surrogate free spirit that keeps the owner safely removed from the bad behavior while permitting him to strut around the streets of Manhattan with caveman bravado. Most owners fall somewhere between these extremes. Harry is more of an *Apologizer* than an *Apologist.* His is a sensitive, tender nature inside that rugged and imposing frame. Once he had waited hours for tickets to Shakespeare's *Cymbeline* at the Delacorte Theater in the park only to come home empty-handed. The tickets had been for Imogen (Harry, needless to say, is not the consummate theatergoer). A whole day had been wasted that he could have spent painting. Another man might have been annoyed, but Harry took Imogen out to dinner and got back on the ticket line even earlier the next day. Harry can be untutored but remains deeply civilized because he possesses that civilizing trait: he can forget himself for others.

Harry let me off my leash and I snuffled around an oak tree, drawing the layers of smell deep into my olfactories. Ah, a dog's nose in the dirt. If I begin to wax about this wonder, I might not stop and there is a story to tell. I was about to push my snout beneath another root in search of a smell trail richer and more beguiling than the bouquet of a fine burgundy wine when

Harry began to shout.

"Randolph, we've got trouble. Here comes Daisy Mae."

All thoughts of olfactory delights vanished. In a more perfect world, the name *Daisy Mae* would not evoke fear and a perilously fast heartbeat. In a more perfect world, though, the name would never be attached to a female Great Dane with a penchant for male Labradors of well-above-average intelligence.

"Run for it," Harry said.

My owner, caught between the charging monster and me, put up the best defense he could given the enemy was nearly two hundred pounds and moving at twenty miles an hour. He jumped into the tree and managed to grab the lowest branch. But this did him little good. Daisy Mae paused for a moment in her pursuit of Yours Truly, reared back on her hind legs and planted her front legs on his chest. Harry had played water polo in college. He has strong arms and a very powerful grip. He held fast. Daisy Mae didn't knock him down, instead he swung back and forth like a piñata in a hurricane. The Great Dane drenched him with her enormous tongue before resuming her quest for finer prey. Some stubborn instinct had made it impossible for me to run as my owner instructed. We Labradors are a committed and faithful lot, and I could no more leave Harry hanging from a tree limb than let an apple fritter go to waste.

Before I too was bowled over by the Great Dane, though, a sharp command issued from the darkness.

"Stop this instant, Daisy Mae."

The great beast turned her massive head toward the speaker.

"Now."

Daisy Mae slowed to a walk. Harry and I had encountered this Amazon during the morning and afternoon, but never at night. During the day, Harriet walked Daisy Mae. Harriet was a professional dog walker and took care of several of our neighborhood's dogs when their owners were at work. She was fifty-something, kind-eyed and dangerously outgunned by her charges, who often competed among themselves to bring the poor woman down. Daisy Mae never paid any heed to Harriet.

But the voice that stilled the Great Dane now was something entirely different. It belonged to a female but wasn't really feminine at all.

"Dammit, you big oaf. I'll make you pay."

Daisy Mae began to whimper and look helpless — a feat for an animal as heavy as a walnut armoire. The woman who emerged out of the darkness wore a smile, but there was nothing friendly about it. I had seen this kind of expression before, usually on the faces of Manhattan's designer-clad and cell-phone dependent elite. It was a symbol of pleasantness over something acidic and critical, a tight expression, always qualified by a certain tension at the corner of the eyes and mouth.

"She just adores men — like her mommy," the woman said.

She snapped a leash onto Daisy Mae's collar.

Harry dropped from the tree.

"Are you her mommy?" Harry asked.

"Her mommy and her meal ticket."

The woman stepped into a small circle of lamplight and I could see her face more clearly. Anatomically it was a pretty face, even a soft face, listing gently into late middle age. But the hardness beneath the smile was unmistakable.

"I thought your dog was one of those pigs that dig for truffles the way he was shoveling his nose in the dirt," she said, making what she must have thought was a humorous reference to my earlier interest in the soil at the base of the oak.

"Yeah, Randolph likes to get into things,"

Harry said.

The woman gave me a rubdown with a gloved hand.

"He's a meaty one," she said.

I would have recoiled on principle had the sensation not been so pleasant. Unfortunately, we Labradors are sometimes slaves to our lower natures. Daisy Mae, meanwhile, was sitting down on her wide haunches and looking utterly serene.

"Haven't we met?" Harry asked.

"I'm quite sure we have not."

"Last night. At the séance," Harry said. "Weren't you there?"

"Please don't mention it. The past twenty-four hours have been an absolute nightmare."

"So you were there?"

"I hardly knew the man and he decided to die in my house. I have no interest in the occult or any such nonsense, but my friend insisted."

"Iris?" Harry asked.

"Yes, Iris. She organized it. Couldn't have the thing at her place. She lives in a rent-controlled studio in the eighties. Charming I suppose, if you want to cohabit with books and roaches."

"Was Iris Overton's ex-wife?" Harry asked.

"Whatever made you think that?" Daisy Mae's owner asked.

"She nagged him."

"She had a wife complex. Overton never married her. She knew him before he was married — badly smitten. Then he met the other woman. Iris took it hard. He called the other woman his true love — whatever that means — and married her instead. His true love dies on their wedding night, he publicly declares that he will never remarry, forty years pass. Iris doesn't move on either. Overton turns the topic of his dead wife into a minor literary industry. Then, out of the blue, a few months ago, Overton calls her and they're a couple again — she's as stupid as they come when it comes to men."

The woman stopped to catch her breath.

"My name's Beatrice."

She extended her hand to Harry. "And you?"

"Harry."

"So what were you doing there?" Beatrice asked.

"I was invited to assist at the séance."

My owner made it sound as if he was constantly assisting at séances when, in fact, this was his first such experience and the invitation, as I have already recounted, had come unsigned in the mail with no return address. Madame Sosostris, it had claimed, was prone to faint when she was in her trances and could Harry please attend to her as an assistant.

"You take that nonsense seriously?" Beatrice jangled Daisy Mae's leash.

"It isn't nonsense."

"To each his own. The whole thing's been very disruptive and I wish I had never agreed to play host. Overton could have had his heart attack somewhere else and I wouldn't have had my apartment turned into a disaster area."

"So it was a heart attack?"

"There hasn't been an autopsy yet. There will be, of course. If you die suddenly the coroner has to take a look at you no matter what — but what else could it be? He had a history of heart problems. Iris told me he wore a pacemaker and his blood pressure was stratospheric. Though, according to her, it didn't seem to slow him down in the sack."

"He *was* relatively young," Harry said.

"His best days were behind him. I think it's a small mercy for a man like that to die before he sees just how irrelevant he is."

"I didn't see Daisy Mae at your apartment last night," Harry said.

"Her ladyship?" Beatrice said, clipping the

dog's ear with her hand. "She stays locked in the bedroom when company comes."

"But I'm sure I met you," Harry said.

"Not a chance," Beatrice said quickly. "I left before it began."

Daisy Mae had been silent since Beatrice had called her off, but at these words she grew animated. As I have mentioned, communicating with my kind is almost always a struggle. Daisy Mae was no exception. The intelligible word was hidden in a verbal briar patch of whines, huffs and loud tongue wagging.

But the Great Dane's intelligible word was significant.

"Liar," Daisy Mae said. "Liar, liar, liar."

I didn't have a chance to learn more. But the word matched the great, contradictory cloud of smells around Beatrice that my nose was absorbing — old leather, black pepper, coconut, figs and roses.

"I'd better be going," Harry said.

"Of course you must."

Beatrice reached down to stroke my head. The smells grew stronger and stronger and more and more complex, overwhelming my capacity to keep them straight (perhaps I should append a chart). In brief: old leather was the smell of an old lie; coconut that of a more recent deception; and wildflowers told of the antic red-herring weave of a daydream. But there was also another very distinct smell emanating from the tips of Beatrice's fingers: burnt wires.

And my nose shoveled in a substantial sample when Beatrice gave my ear a hard squeeze and began to withdraw with Daisy Mae. Harry attached my leash and pulled me in the opposite direction.

"Until we meet again," Beatrice said as she walked into the night.

One Word on the Canine Olfactories Vague Suspicions Grow

Burnt wires were just the beginning. Let's take a moment to talk about dogs and smells by way of an illuminating digression.

A recent study by a group of British scientists has discovered what my kind has always known: dogs can smell cancer.

The study employed a dozen canines to perform the undignified task of sniffing urine samples from both the sick and the well. The dogs were able to determine the cancer samples with a high level of accuracy. The text of the study is filled with fascinating anecdotes. The scientists relate incident after incident in which average dogs revealed an amazing capacity to detect disease in their owners. In one instance, a woman approached a doctor to have a mole removed. Her dog, it seemed, was obsessed with the growth and repeatedly tried to bite it off even while he ignored her other moles. The mole, the doctor determined, was a malignant melanoma, a deadly form of skin cancer. Thanks to the insistent pet, which the study saw fit to keep anonymous and uncredited (typical), the woman lived.

I have already alluded to a dog's sense of smell being 100,000 times that of humans, but, as suggested by the cancer study, dogs don't just detect everyday scents better; they smell things that aren't even thought of as smells. I have heard it said of dogs that we can smell fear. This doesn't go far enough. Not only can I smell fear, I smell variations and micro-variations of almost every human emotion. It takes a very great discipline of mind to encounter, analyze and order this constant barrage of scents and an even greater discipline — one lacking in most dogs — to think and act logically in the face of what amounts to permanent odor intoxication. If Harry is thinking about Imogen, I can smell these thoughts: rosemary, cantaloupe, pine, rain and the sea. If he is debating what to have for lunch, I can smell this too: usually a toss-up between a chicken parm and a roast beef sandwich with extra mayo.

That is why, even before Daisy Mae called Beatrice a liar, I had already begun to process several scent clues that made me doubt Beatrice's veracity. From the moment we met Beatrice, she had been shedding heavy doses of anxiety, suspicion, anger, temper, dishonesty and potential violence, as well as a deep dislike of males — a scent especially pungent at the moment Beatrice verbally suggested the opposite by saying that she "adored" men. All of these markers passed through my quivering nostrils and into my thoughts. The scents were as thick as if she had doused herself with a perfume made of them. Beyond the old leather and the coconut were hints of vanilla and cinnamon, cloves and almonds. The bouquet of fresh tobacco leaves and grass clashed with the bitterness of an old ashtray. They grew even more profound when the conversation turned to Overton. The emotions — especially anxiety — reached their highest pitch when Beatrice discussed the city's requirement for an autopsy. Was she afraid of what might be found? Beatrice was not the woman she presented herself to be — who she actually was and what that meant about Overton's demise remained to be seen.

But my profound snout has its limitations. There is a term that military strategists use: the fog of war. The fog of war means the practical impossibility of seeing clearly in a situation that contains numerous variables all unfolding in a chaotic theater. The variables give birth to variables, they in turn give birth to more variables. The old leather of an old lie becomes impossible to pin down on any time line without other facts and correlations. The coconut of a fresh lie could point to serious deceit or just a fib. There are other scents that qualify the main scents and each category has a dozen sub-categories. Such is the condition when I inhale a rich shovelful of odor like I did with Beatrice at the dog run. My head can spin, my brain get overwhelmed, smells can settle into the unconscious and only later will I make an important connection. Only later, will Yours Truly proclaim: *Aha, I understand!*

CHRISTMAS AT JACKSON'S
A GUATEMALAN TREE SLOTH PROVIDES A REASON TO FEAR

We didn't encounter Beatrice or Daisy Mae again in the short time before Christmas.

The autopsy results were reported in the newspaper on Christmas Eve and they confirmed Beatrice's assumption: Overton had died of a fatal arrhythmia. His heart had started beating irregularly and then stopped beating altogether. The question of why his pacemaker seemed to have failed was raised briefly and the newspaper suggested the possibility of a defect, going so far as to print that phone calls to the manufacturer had gone unanswered by press time. That an autopsy had revealed no evidence of foul play did not mean that foul play had not occurred. An absence of evidence is not evidence of absence.

Of course, nothing was clear to me, but a few things at least were percolating in my mind — not the least among them Imogen's code. I managed to make some preparatory

progress with $_{12}$*CDYZMNBCEFLMIJNOEF8$_9$*.
Fortunately, Imogen had kept a small volume entitled *A Practical Guide to Everyday Cryptography* on the second shelf of the bookcase — easily reachable via snout-swipe. This handy work, attained by my mistress for twenty-five cents from the bookstalls around Washington Square Park, explained the basics of breaking codes. In it I learned about *ciphers* (a method for encrypting messages). Encrypting is simply the transformation of a message into something that cannot be readily understood by an unintended party. The original message is called the *clear* or the *plaintext* and the encrypted message is called alternatively the *ciphertext* or the *cryptogram.* I waded into heady discussions of the *Gronsfeld Cipher,* which I learned was a variation of the *Vigenere Cipher* and the *McMurphy Conundrum,* a variation of the *Brandeis Enigma . . .* All this initial exploration had occurred just in that first night. Now less than two days later, my brain still labored, attempting to tabulate a solution to these twenty-two characters jotted down in an obvious hurry by my mistress just hours before her disappearance. But I will talk more about my efforts and the workings of the cipher systems later.

Harry wasn't going home for Christmas. His parents had applied copious quantities of encouragement and stiff doses of guilt but nothing could move their son to return to Milwaukee. He said it was a matter of kenneling me, but when they hinted at coming East to New York to be with him, Harry had discouraged them. Eventually they gave up and booked a senior citizens' cruise to Cozumel.

This meant one thing, Harry and I were going to have Christmas dinner at Jackson's. Jackson is the closest thing to a mentor and benefactor Harry has. He is a Southern transplant of atmospheric wealth who has lived in a suite at the Belvedere Hotel for the past twenty-eight years. The wealth came from a family business that manufactured suppositories, a fortune, as Jackson phrased it, that was built on a firm foundation. Before Imogen disappeared and Harry entered a wasteland of sadness and broken expectations, my owner was a promising painter. He had shown his work in Tribeca, was gaining a modest following and media attention. On the strength of this he met Jackson.

Jackson Temple had earned his PhD in art history from Princeton. He is a Rubens expert and has written an important study of the artist. When an overexuberant reviewer had described Harry as a modern-day Rubens, Jackson had naturally taken a look. He liked what he saw and bought some paintings. Harry and Jackson became friends and eventually Jackson began paying our rent and other expenses. Imogen had also been fond of Jackson and Jackson of her. When she had disappeared, Jackson had gone so far as to buy advertising time on New York television to help find her. It was Jackson who instructed Harry to take a break from painting when my owner wanted to lose himself in his art only two months after Imogen disappeared. I think that Jackson regretted this advice after Harry met Ivan Manners and sent his restless energy into paranormal investigation. But Jackson had never raised the subject with my owner — instead, gentleman that he was, he always offered Harry a place to put up his feet and have a good meal.

Manhattan was still when we ventured out just before noon on Christmas Day. Harry had decided to wrap a red velvet bow of absurd proportions around my neck and don a Santa Claus hat himself.

"Might as well make the best of it," Harry grumbled as the front door closed behind us.

The day was frigid and gray. We walked the several blocks to the Belvedere. Once Harry paused below the expansive lower window of a brownstone to stare into its warm interior. A Christmas tree stood in the corner of the living room and a fire blazed in the hearth around which the stockings of this fortunate family were hung. Nothing would be easy for Harry today.

I didn't have the heart to pull on my leash and break his reverie, which, of course, was also my own. A woman came to the window, saw Harry staring into her living room, and went to get her husband. Even on Christmas Day — a day when the most radically generous love is thought to swaddle the earth — we creatures can't seem to do anything but cleave to our own little fiefdoms and spheres of safety and concern. Fair enough, I suppose. Even those people most familiar to us are mysteries and carry risk (that included Imogen, as well now). When the couple returned, Harry got the message and moved on.

Visitors are announced at the Belvedere. As usual the concierge gave us both a doubtful look before picking up the phone and dialing our host.

"Dogs aren't allowed," he said as we made our way to the elevator. "But for Mr. Temple exceptions must be made."

Jackson's suite is clean but cluttered. In fact, the space is so cluttered that one must navigate through piles of vertically stacked books and great clumps of rolled canvases propped against walls and sticking out from closets. This Christmas, the situation was even more dire, since Jackson had seen fit to stand a fourteen-foot double balsam in the center of the main room. In Jackson fashion, the tree remained undecorated and listed gravely to one side.

"Welcome, my friends," Jackson said. "*Joyeux Noel. Froeliche Weinachten.* I have ordered something called a traditional feast from Dean & DeLuca. Though I don't see what's so traditional about it, the yams have been polluted by marshmallows."

My olfactories swam with the indescribable delight of roast beef, Yorkshire pudding and, yes, even yams with marshmallows. Jackson took Harry's coat and my leash and draped them over a ceramic fountain in the far corner. He poured my owner a glass of sherry and led both of us to a vacant space near the tree that he had somehow reclaimed from the general disorder.

"To peace in our world and in our hearts — but not too much peace. Too much peace atrophies the soul," Jackson said.

"How goes it?" Harry asked.

"It goes, my boy, it goes. Marlin has a fungal infection between his toes, and I am being sued for libel in connection with an article I published in an academic journal."

"How are you, Marlin?" Harry called over to the Guatemalan tree sloth inching his way ever higher in the ficus tree by the window. Marlin turned his head in my owner's direction and blinked.

"Who did you libel?" Harry asked.

"A little man determined to be king of the Rubens's world and I refuse to be dethroned. The egos of some people, especially tenured people. He actually took offense at the phrase 'maestro of lechery.' "

"Applied to Rubens?"

"Oh no, my boy. Applied to him. You can't sue on behalf of the long dead."

"Aren't you worried, Jackson?"

"Not really. I have been sued by academics before and I have never lost. As long as what I write is true, I can't lose. What I write about Rubens might be speculation and downright falsehood, but what I write about living people must always be true. This little man has never met a college freshman of either sex he didn't like. How about opening some presents?"

Jackson handed Harry two parcels.

"One is for you and the other is for Randolph."

Harry's present was a paintbrush.

"A paintbrush," Harry said.

"Not just any paintbrush, my boy. This one comes with a commission."

"Thank you, I think."

"We'll talk about it after we've filled our tanks. Open Randolph's."

"I'm sorry I didn't get anything for Marlin," Harry said.

"Marlin has his tree. That's enough for Mr. Marlin."

Harry handed Jackson a box of chocolates he had bought from Duane Reade.

"I almost forgot," he muttered.

"Thank you. Another what-to-get-the-millionaire-in-your-life moment. You can never have enough cherry cordials. Now, without further ado, please open Randolph's."

Harry unwrapped what looked like a red beach towel.

"A towel?" he asked.

"Look inside the towel."

Harry shook the towel. A golden ticket fell to the floor. He picked it up and read.

"A pool membership for Randolph?" Harry asked.

"No Labrador should be without one.

They are natural swimmers, you know, and a bit more exercise could do this one no harm."

There are two swimming pools in New York for dogs. Jackson had bought me a one-year membership at the Pooch Palace — Canine Pool and Spa in Midtown. Their pool, largely used for canine hydrotherapy, also allows recreational swimming.

"He swam in the boathouse pond once, but a swan attacked him."

"The pool will be ideal then. He can swim to his heart's content and fear neither shark nor swan. And — you will note — Randolph has also been enrolled in a canine yoga class. It meets weekdays at some ungodly hour."

Canine yoga, I thought, what next? Swimming was a welcome treat, but I have never been particularly flexible. What next, indeed. Fortunately, roast beef, Yorkshire pudding and yams with marshmallows were next.

Our host managed to roll a room service cart heaped with the steaming goodies within our reach.

"I'll serve your dog first. He looks more appreciative than either of us."

Jackson, who has always been sympathetic to my appetites, loaded a plate with ample helpings of meat and the doughy, buttery pudding for which I have a particular fondness.

I waited until everyone had been served before beginning to eat.

"This is extraordinary. No animal I know would stand on ceremony like our Randolph," Jackson said.

"Imogen's doing," Harry said between mouthfuls.

"Harry, I've never interfered . . ."

"But you might now?"

"Not if it's still too raw."

"It's as raw as it was the day she went away."

Jackson returned to his meal. Harry stared at his hands.

"I'm sorry, Jackson."

"Don't fret, my boy."

We finished eating in silence. Jackson patted Harry on the shoulder and rose to his feet.

"Allow me to set the plum pudding on fire."

After several attempts, Jackson ignited the brandy-soaked ball.

"Voilà," Jackson said, swinging the burning dessert dangerously close to the Christmas tree.

Sometime later he brought out cigars and a bottle of port.

"I feel very old boyish," Jackson said.

He expelled a great cloud of smoke into the room.

"Speaking of old boys, I lost one of my number from the prep this week. Lyell Overton Minskoff-Hardy. He was famous for all the wrong reasons."

Harry leaned forward intently.

"I was there."

"Where?"

"In the bathroom."

"When he died?" Jackson asked. "Now that *is* interesting."

"Actually, I thought that maybe you were the connection," Harry said. "I got a letter in the mail telling me to attend."

"Oh no. You've got the wrong man. Have I ever done anything to encourage you in your paranormal investigations?"

"Right," Harry said.

"It was probably one of your friends. Ivan Manners and his parrot. There's a network of those people, isn't there?"

Harry nodded. Jackson's scent was always unflappable, impenetrable, cool — but during this exchange there was a kind of break in the scent. Jackson wasn't saying everything he knew.

"Overton was my third-form roommate at Merton. A nicer boy has never become a less worthy man. What exactly were you doing in his vicinity?"

Harry told him about the séance and Overton's death.

"He died on the floor with his fly open," Harry finished. "He was still alive when I reached him."

"He was?" Jackson asked, once again his unflappable scent was betrayed by an interruption suggesting something just short of worry.

"He said *Elektra,*" Harry reported.

"Elektra?" Jackson sounded mildly puzzled but his scent suggested a growing concern. "You mean after the Sophocles play?"

Harry nodded.

"That's truly bizarre. The newspapers said nothing about this," Jackson said. "He had so much promise when I knew him. I followed his career and from time to time we'd run into each other — but each time the man was more and more a caricature of himself. You could see it in his work. Different subjects, but the same themes and the same central preoccupation — Gabriella, his dead bride. How Gothic and predictable."

"But it was the tragedy of his life," Harry insisted.

"Overton chose it as his tragedy."

"That seems harsh."

"Not if you knew what I knew about the man. He wasn't the lovelorn Edgar Allan Poe widower that he depicted in his books. Indeed, Gabriella's death was a tragedy. But it would have been a larger tragedy if he actually loved her the way he said he did."

"Sounds like slander to me."

"Again, it's only slander if it isn't true and besides he's dead," Jackson said. "Tell me, Harry, was there anyone else there in the bathroom?"

"Iris, the annoying woman," Harry said.

"Ah, yes, Iris. The *annoying* woman," Jackson echoed. This time both sound and scent conveyed a distinct sadness, but only for a moment because Jackson soon changed the subject.

"Let's talk about something else," he exclaimed with forced mirth. "It's Christmas for God's sake."

There was obviously something that Jackson was not saying, but I did not linger because Marlin had suddenly become agitated. Agitation for a Guatemalan tree sloth is unlike agitation for almost any other creature on the planet save the sea sponge. It is a subtle thing, a very subtle thing. But I pride myself on a general sensitivity to my fellow creatures and have long held to the

Henry Jamesian ideal: "to be a [dog] upon whom nothing is lost." This sensitivity means that if a Guatemalan tree sloth twitches its right ear three times in a minute and accompanies this twitch with two eye blinks and a tail shiver, I know that something is amiss.

I took my leave of Harry and Jackson and waded through chest-high boxes, prints and dusty bottles of Cognac until I reached the base of Marlin's tree.

"Is everything okay?" I asked.

A word on cross-species communication is required: there is a glaring lack in the scientific and/or practical literature on the subject. With the exception of a few electrode-implanted dolphins at SeaWorld, little is known about what, if anything, animals of different species actually say to one another. Everything I know has been limited by the narrow world of my own experience and is the product of hit-or-miss encounters with cockroaches, rats, birds and one Guatemalan tree sloth named Marlin. An animal's outward movements, gestures and general physical impression offer few clues as to the speed, breadth and overall brilliance of its brain. I will use myself as an example. A dog has little muscular control over its face. Mine, set in a permanent mask of blankness, does nothing to suggest the mind within. A distinct lack of control over my salivary glands, tongue and tail make it nearly impossible for me to assume the posture of dignified philosophical reflection. I am like a human in a paralyzed body whose intelligence is contradicted by the uncooperative mechanism that contains the mind. Marlin shares this problem.

Guatemalan tree sloths may very well be one of the most intelligent creatures on earth. Their language is composed of high-pitched blasts of the most condensed information. Imagine a fax machine that transmits a thousand pages a second. Yet their bodies are almost paralytic. In the hour since our arrival at Jackson's, Marlin had managed to climb just two inches and eat three leaves.

The Guatemalan tree sloth did not answer me and I made the mistake of repeating the question.

"Is everything okay?"

At this Marlin's right ear twitched a fourth time and the sonic blasts began.

In the rush of information that followed, thankfully repeated by Marlin in deference to the slower speed of my central processing unit, I learned that Jackson's apartment actually overlooked the apartment in which

Overton had died. Marlin apologized for not pointing, but explained that it would have taken all day. I nuzzled my way between the curtain and Marlin's tree to reach the window. As I looked for the right apartment among the rows and rows of windows, Marlin's description of its interior led me to the right one. It was directly across the street on the same floor though slightly lower. A word on dogs' eyesight (at least *this* dog's eyesight) that runs contrary to general belief: (1) I can see in color and (2) I can see at least as well as Harry. Case in point, the apartment was many feet distant yet I could clearly see the dining room where the séance had been held, parts of the hallway down which Overton had made his last trip to the bathroom and a bedroom. The bedroom arrested my attention. Every inch of its walls was covered with the most amazing tapestries. They seemed to be Indian in origin, traditional hieratic depictions of Hindu gods on lush dark backgrounds. Delicate-looking objects made from glass lined a bureau that ran along one wall and lace curtains on the canopy bed. One would not confine a dog like Daisy Mae in a room like this.

I turned to Marlin. Had the coincidence of proximity to the site of Overton's demise been the reason for Marlin's post-dinner agitation? Another sonic blast informed me that indeed it had not. There was more to the story, my Central American friend said, and I must pay better attention if I hoped to grasp it. Marlin had recognized Harry as a participant at the séance. He had observed the death of Overton and its aftermath. But he had also observed weeks of comings and goings at the apartment across the way.

Indeed, he had seen things that even a Guatemalan tree sloth couldn't make sense of — things that had made Marlin quite afraid.

A Tree Sloth Tells
a Worrisome Tale
A Dog Organizes
the Facts

The volume of the Guatemalan tree sloth's communication overwhelmed my capacity to comprehend. It took several recitations by that very patient creature before I could assemble the following facts in outline form:

1. From his perch in the tree, Marlin had witnessed a man and a woman meeting at the apartment on several occasions and disappearing into the bedroom for unobserved, but suspected, intimacies behind hastily closed drapes. The man was certainly Overton (Marlin identified him from the night of the séance); the woman was likely Iris, Beatrice's friend and Overton's onetime sweetheart. The *annoying* woman . . .

2. From a lower branch that resulted in a partially obstructed view, Marlin observed this same couple arguing fiercely in the late afternoon on the day of the séance. The argument ended when the woman heaved a paperweight shaped like an eggplant in the

general direction of the man. The man, in an effort to avoid the projectile, jumped aside, lost his balance and fell heavily to the floor. The woman quickly rushed to his side and helped him to his feet. The man seemed to have hurt his head on the coffee table. The woman offered an ice pack from the freezer and the man accepted. The couple then disappeared into the bedroom for unobserved, but suspected, intimacies behind hastily closed drapes.

3. Having slipped from the uppermost branch of the tree onto the nearby drape (to hang there until rescue by Jackson), stalwart Marlin nonetheless witnessed, two days prior to this fight, a visit by a workman carrying a toolbox and a large cardboard container. The workman, who was greeted by the woman with a prolonged kiss on the lips, entered the bathroom to emerge some time later with the toolbox and a flattened cardboard container. The couple then disappeared into the bedroom for unobserved, but suspected, intimacies behind hastily closed drapes.

These episodic observations had interested Marlin much like watching a soap opera with no sound — a distant drama with no real impact on his life. And then came the night of Overton's demise. Two hours after the séance participants, police and ambulance personnel had disbanded in the chaotic aftermath of Overton's death, the Guatemalan tree sloth saw something that made this distant drama uncomfortably close:

4. Marlin's very own Jackson Temple slipped into the apartment. Jackson was unable to turn on the lights, but proceeded to the bathroom and emerged soon after, agitated and carrying a shopping bag. As he entered the living room on his way to the front door, a woman whom Marlin said was a frequent visitor to the apartment arrived and confronted him. Jackson pushed the woman violently against the bookcase. Marlin had never known his owner to be anything but a consummate gentleman, yet he could not deny the evidence of his eyes. Jackson collected the shopping bag and left the apartment. The woman slid to the floor and began to sob. Jackson did not return to the suite until well after midnight and went directly to bed. Marlin's detailed description of the woman made me believe that she was Beatrice.

Guatemalan tree sloths are calm by necessity. Their natural habitat is filled with predators who would gladly snap them up for an appetizer but for the promise of their foul-tasting flesh. Imagine being in a state of near paralysis, surrounded by hungry meat eaters, who you hope know that you taste unpleasant and going on with your life just the same. You will then understand why Marlin was not easy to upset. But the discovery of a different side to his long-term owner proved deeply disturbing. Again, I found an outline helpful:

1. In this world of slavery and servitude that is the reality for most pets, Marlin understood that his well-being depended upon his owner's continued freedom. If his owner was involved in some kind of illegal activity, then his owner ran the risk of arrest and Marlin ran the risk of an undetermined change in his circumstances with personal extinction as a possible consequence.

2. Marlin had a deep affection for Jackson, built on years of sharing the same suite at the Belvedere and his long ago rescue from the clutches of a disreputable petting zoo. He had come to know the man as admittedly eccentric but enormously generous and thoughtful. But there could be no mistaking that Jackson had committed the violent action against the woman in the apartment across the way. Attempting to reconcile this fact with what he knew of his owner had left the Guatemalan tree sloth in

a state of turmoil.

3. It now seemed quite possible to Marlin that Jackson might do him harm. If his owner could shove a woman against a wall so easily, what would stop him from dispatching his own pet? Certainly not Marlin's foul-tasting flesh or herbivore's limp bite.

The creature also imparted several other curious facts:

1. Daisy Mae was neither an inhabitant of the apartment in question nor a visitor;

2. the woman Marlin had seen on the day of the séance, who I believed was Beatrice, did not live in the apartment; and

3. Madame Sosostris, the clairvoyant who had run the séance, actually knocked with her knee on the underside of the table to simulate spiritual answers. The old fraud had sat with her back to the window in plain view of the Guatemalan tree sloth.

Marlin's revelations left me shaken. Foul play seemed even more likely now in Overton's death and the need to learn of any connection to Imogen's disappearance had become much more urgent.

After sunset, Harry rose from the couch. My owner had indulged in several after dinner drinks while Marlin and I had conversed and his balance was unsteady.

"Do you want me to call a car?" Jackson

asked. "The car service never takes longer than five minutes to arrive."

Harry waved off the offer.

"I'm fine," he said. "I'm going to enjoy the walk."

I bid good-bye to Marlin who replied with an anxious transmission.

"Good night *not* good-bye," I corrected as reassuringly as I could, which given my canine limitations meant making a clearing of the throat sound. To those in the know it is taken as a compassionate vote of support.

The concierge was nowhere to be seen when we reached the lobby. A portable television filled the air with the static-heavy notes of *The Nutcracker.* Harry pushed through the glass and steel doors of the lobby with a great sigh. The air was crisp and a light snow had begun to fall. Already the cars parked along the curb were skimmed white. Hardly anyone was about as we made our way up the street past vivid yellow windows toward Central Park West.

Harry had purchased another pack of cigarettes and had designated them his new emergency cigarettes. I suppose that he felt — as did I — like we inhabited a kind of perpetual emergency. As was his custom, he had hidden the emergency cigarettes away in the kitchen only to bring them out almost immediately and begin the process of demolishing their contents. He extracted a cigarette and lit it.

"That was a great dinner, wasn't it, Randolph?" Harry mused and dragged the smoke deep into his lungs.

I could not get used to seeing my owner smoke. He had never done so when Imogen had been with us. The habit had begun in the first weeks after her disappearance when a sleepless Harry found himself surrounded by a ragtag bunch of nicotine-driven friends and volunteers, all rallying around our lost mistress. It had grown naturally out of the desperation of those days and had settled into a kind of prop for the broken backdrop of weeks and months that followed — the broken backdrop that had now become our life.

When Harry and I reached Central Park West, my owner decided to cross the avenue. The other side was dark and desolate. The snow began to fall more steadily and the wind picked up to a stiff clip pushing us home. Harry swayed north slowly while I did my best to avoid the patches of snow-melting salt that get caught in my paws and cause much discomfort.

Halfway home, I looked up for a moment and received a shock. With the wind blowing from behind, I could smell nothing of what lay ahead on the footpath but what I saw sent my full-body canine alarm system into high alert from head to tail. A strange ghostly figure of enormous proportions stood two blocks ahead of us. I could not tell if the figure was man or woman. Given its size and clothing — a massive heavy-weather coat topped by a rancher's hat — I thought it was more man than woman, but at the same time even from that distance I thought I could detect a certain feminine softness. The sight was so strange that at first I thought I was imagining things, but my defensive senses being the reliable mechanisms they are, and this being Manhattan — an island prone to eccentrics — I concluded that not only was this spectral figure very real but it was waiting for *us*. I stopped dead in my tracks.

"Randolph, what the hell are you doing?" Harry said, slurring his words. Far from growing more sober in the cold night air, the last few drinks were now making themselves felt and my owner was fast approaching a disappointingly sloppy state of inebriation.

"Crazy mutt," Harry continued sense-lessly, forgetting that I am a purebred. My owner yanked my leash, but I stood my ground. For a moment, I felt a pang of compassion for those pets both dog and other who must endure an alcoholic owner. Harry yanked the leash again much harder but it slipped from his hand and fell to the ground. He slumped down onto the sidewalk after it, searching the snow for the loop.

"Goddamn it, Randolph. You know how to pick 'em, don't you?"

The figure had begun to walk toward us. There was something death-like about it and the shimmering quality of the lamp-lit falling snow made the figure even more menacing. Everything about the figure told me that it wanted Harry . . . that my owner was its target. There is a misconception about dogs that we don't sweat. True, we don't sweat much, but we are able to perspire between our toes, and when overheated or scared, believe me, we do.

Harry fumbled around in the snow, dropping the pack of emergency cigarettes into a slushy puddle along with the cigarette he was smoking. I faced the approaching figure, preparing to charge it and sweated between my toes. But then I was granted a reprieve.

"Goddamn, Randolph, now I've got to go all the way over to Broadway and buy another pack." Harry rose to his feet.

The figure was less than a block away now. I began to whimper in an attempt to hurry Harry along.

"You're not going to like this, pudgy," Harry said, glancing at his watch, "but we're going to take a little jog. *Christmas Hauntings* starts in fifteen minutes and I swear I am *not* going to miss it."

For once, I didn't mind either the insult or the faster pace. My owner sprinted back across the avenue and down a side street toward Broadway. A few blocks later we came to a stop in front of a bodega. The figure was gone.

Dog Turns Detective and Plots His Next Move A Bowl of Cereal Becomes A Bridge Between Species

Marlin's story, the threatening figure and all the other revelations of the past few days weighed heavily on me that night. Harry watched his television program about ghosts and I brooded about real world dangers. Should I show my owner the journal? Share Marlin's revelations? Somehow communicate the still murky possibility that Imogen and Overton and this threatening figure were all related?

I had always been aware of my limitations in this world run by bipeds, but now these limitations seemed dangerous. I shared the tree sloth's sense of powerlessness. A dog has no civil rights. He cannot traipse around the city streets on his own unless he fancies a trip to the pound. A dog has no historical precedent, no basis for being appreciated as anything but a mute, vaguely intelligent companion. At law, we remain chattel, protected by bleeding hearts and local ordinance, but ultimately we are property — property to be bought, sold and disposed of. Take a bite out of someone's pant leg or go incontinent and it's eternal night for my kind. I was ill equipped to protect Marlin, defend Harry or even preserve myself.

Somehow I needed to enlist Harry. I considered, but rejected, trying to put Imogen's journal in front of him — it needed context. But how to give the journal context without letting Harry know that I had an unusually fine brain? I had never attempted to make Harry understand that I was sentient for one crucial reason — albeit a vaguely paranoid one. Even good-hearted Harry would be tempted to share this fact with the world and Yours Truly might end up with electrodes connected to his cerebral cortex or under the vivisectionist's knife. Perhaps a modern day P. T. Barnum might recruit me for a touring freak show.

Fortunately, my owner is like so many twenty- and thirtysomethings. He clings to childish things. In Harry's case, Alpha-Bits cereal is that thing. Alpha-Bits is cereal in the shape of all the letters of the English alphabet from A–Z. Because of the randomness of these alphabetic bits and the law of probability, these letters rarely form words that have any meaning — quite unlike the cereal's preposterous television commercials in which they spell out promotional slogans for the product.

The morning after our visit to Jackson's, Harry stumbled out of bed and sat down at our cluttered kitchen table. His nose was deep in a book entitled *The Workings of the Spirit Mind; Why Their Logic Defies Ours (And How to Get Around It)*. Harry had finished his first bowl of Alpha-Bits and was about to pour another, when he began to peer into the bottom of his bowl.

"Amazing," my owner said. "They really are always trying to communicate."

He held the bowl closer to his face. Apparently a word had formed in the bottom that arrested my owner's attention. He spelled it aloud.

"*L-O-G-E-C.* Logec. Obviously logic misspelled. Part of the title is the word *logic. Why Their Logic Defies Ours . . .*"

Harry refilled his bowl with cereal and then to my ample embarrassment used his spoon to write *UNDERSTOOD* with the letters. He waited several minutes for his soggy breakfast to respond. When it didn't, he returned to his book.

Eureka, I exclaimed in a strangled bark-sneeze complete with body wiggle, tail wag and collar jingle. In that very instant, my problem had been solved.

"Calm down, Randolph," Harry said. "You'll have a heart attack."

But I had reason to rejoice. Alpha-Bits would be my bridge to Harry. My bridge between species. I would use the letters to spell out instructions from the "spirit world" for Harry to follow; supply him with leads and criminal hypotheses; give him insights into those I suspected and suggest whatever else was necessary. As much as I disliked encouraging Harry in his super-natural beliefs, I realized that the Alpha-Bits solution was the best way to get to the bottom of things. It would be no mean feat to make my uncoordinated body arrange cereal letters into messages from the spirit world. But if Vesalius could map the circulatory system, da Vinci draw the perfect circle with his free hand, then Randolph could set his snout and clumsy paws to this good work.

There was really no time to waste. I had hoped to compose my first message by evening, but to do this I needed to be alone and Harry showed no signs of leaving the apartment (which wasn't a bad thing either given what or who might be lying in wait for him). I resigned myself to working overnight in darkness. I went over the plan. Harry always left the cereal box on the table — it was one of his staple foods. I would simply climb up onto the closest chair, tip the box over, shake it until some letters emerged and begin.

But at six o'clock, Harry surprised me by leaving the house to buy something at Duane Reade. The errand promised a solid twenty minutes to experiment. I climbed up onto the chair and leaned across the table, stretching toward the cereal box. I soon realized that this was going to be harder than I had imagined. The box was in the center and I was forced to put more and more weight on the table as I leaned in toward it.

The table began to tilt. I thought it would recover if I backed off the edge. I was wrong. The table and I tumbled onto the floor spilling everything about in a slurry of Alpha-Bits, orange juice, butter and toast. This was an unpromising turn of events. I rolled myself dry on the carpet and dragged the cereal box to a clear patch of floor that I hoped would be prominent enough to catch Harry's attention. After shaking a generous heap of letters out of the box, I began to nose one after the other into a line. This was hard labor. The starchy letters had a tendency to stick to my nose and crumble under my paws. I lost a third of the letters just trying to get them to my message space and another third as I struggled to place them right side up. But this was merely time-consuming. As the work progressed I grew more confident of ultimate success. All I needed was an uninterrupted hour.

But an hour would not be granted. Harry's unmistakable clump-clump grew louder on the stairs. I had two options, both of them bad. I could race to finish my first message and hope that Harry would accept it. Or I could scrap the attempt, roll around in the Alpha-Bits and make it seem that the whole thing was an accident caused by his clumsy dog. Pride — and the thought that the Alpha-Bits would be permanently locked away — prevented me from the latter. I nudged the last letter into place just as the second lock turned. I hurried to my corner and curled up. Then the front door swung open.

"What a mess," Harry said.

He threw his jacket onto the sofa.

"Randolph. Come here."

I acted as if I was awakening from a long nap. I stretched, shook and leaned far back on my haunches. I sauntered over to my owner and looked up at him with innocent eyes.

Then Harry noticed the message on the floor.

MORE TO OVERT DEATH

I could tell by Harry's tone that he had already made the leap into the supernatural. The cereal message would be attributed to forces from beyond.

"That's not good English."

I had not counted on his grammatical pickiness or lack of imagination. Harry is no idiot, but he is a visual artist first and a logical thinker last. He had no impulse to connect Overton's recent death to *overt,* an abbreviation that I had employed to finish quickly. Harry spent the next fifteen minutes speaking various word combinations aloud as he righted the table and cleaned up the spill.

Then he came to a conclusion.

"Overt's an adjective, not a verb. The spirits must mean *a*vert."

The message now read:

MORE TO AVERT DEATH

"Do more to prevent people from dying,"

Harry said.

A noble lesson, I reflected, if wrong — a sort of paranormal public service announcement to counter a population explosion among the dead. But I was not to be defeated. Harry poured the remaining Alpha-Bits onto the table and opened a fresh box. He poured these out as well until there was a mountain of cereal in the middle of the table.

"Tell me anything you want," Harry said to his imagined spectral audience.

He hazarded the refrigerator for a soda, found a stray emergency cigarette behind a banana and returned to the table to sit, smoke and watch. He remained like this for close to an hour, but of course nothing happened.

And then Harry began to sob. He sobbed without inhibition. He howled. He spat. He slammed his fist on the table. Only his dog was watching, but even so, it was the first time his dog had ever seen him cry.

In my eagerness to communicate with my owner, I had overlooked who Harry would think was contacting him from the spirit world. Now there could be no mistake. He was sobbing Imogen's name.

"Imogen. I'm listening," Harry said. "I'm listening, Imogen."

In the many months since she had gone missing, I had never heard my owner suggest that Imogen was dead. I had missed how Harry perceived things. All of the supernatural reading, the association with the absurd Ivan Manners, the séances, all of it was directed to one end: to hear from her just one more time.

I rested my chin on his knee. I felt very cruel.

"Randolph," Harry said, "what the hell is wrong with this world?"

I felt like a carnival huckster who had sold another jackpot chance to someone who could not afford it. The depth of my owner's need for answers and the possibilities the supernatural held for him had never struck me with the power that it did now. I had no idea how much Harry depended on the hope that some key might be found that would unlock Imogen from the enchanted cage in which he believed she must be a prisoner. I felt ashamed to traffic in those hopes but even more ashamed to recognize that on some level I had simply accepted, long ago, the likelihood that the profound, whimsical and vivid human being that was my mistress could have become another drowning victim, another floater in the Hudson, another corpse and her spirit obliterated entirely from the universe. Did my brain really have to be such an enemy of hope? Of course, my dog's body often told me something different. My dog's body often told me that my mistress was alive in both body and soul, but I dismissed this as a holdover from my more primitive canine genes.

"You're a good dog, Randolph. But your owner's a moron," Harry finally said.

He gave my ears a vigorous rub.

"But I can't help it. I keep seeing Imogen walk in that door with a baguette that's 356 days old. Remember how she was late for everything? Missed planes, birthdays, video rentals always racking up the fines . . . I keep imagining her saying: *Would you believe it, I'm getting worse? This time it took me a whole year just to buy bread.*"

We stayed like that for a long time. Boy and dog. Dog and boy. Harry sobbing and muttering. My chin resting on his knee until the well ran dry and Harry decided to take me for a walk.

ANOTHER VISIT TO THE BULL MOOSE DOG RUN AN ADULT EDUCATION BROCHURE REVEALS ITS MANY WONDERS

Initially I was a little jumpy leaving the security of our apartment, half-expecting the menacing figure to emerge from the shadows at any moment. But instead a more mundane challenge arose.

When we reached the courtesy doggy-pickup bag dispenser a short time later, we found that the owner of a King Charles spaniel had beaten us by a few steps and taken the last bag. In New York, humans must pick up after their dogs or risk a hefty fine. Our block association, the loose group of citizens who manage to keep our street orderly and garbage free, had installed a bag dispenser on the sidewalk. Unfortunately, it is so popular that the bags often run out and force dog owners to resort to other less pleasant measures.

"Sorry," the man said plainly not sorry at all as he yanked the bag from its holder.

"That's okay," Harry said.

"It's not the end of the world. Sugar and I have found the Learning Center brochures work great for going potty. Haven't we, Sugar?"

Sugar, a mean-tempered thing with a filthy mouth, snarled at Harry and told me that I was so fat that only tapeworm would help. Sugar's owner continued about the brochure:

"They're glossy so they don't leak and, better still, they're double-stapled."

We walked in the direction of the Learning Center brochure box. A Learning Center brochure is a potpourri of adult education opportunities presented in brash full color to drive the lazy and directionless off their couches and into the lecture hall. For an "amazingly low fee," people who have "made it" will regale the pathetic hordes with tales of their success. The word *success* is used in every listing, whether it is a lecture on writing a best seller, closing a real estate deal or cleansing one's colon. One can learn from political power brokers or become an instant oil painter; make gift baskets that sell like hotcakes or find employment as a personal organizer to the stars. What has always baffled me about the brochures was how the Learning Center managed to recruit anyone, let alone celebrities, to do this questionable work. Harry was obviously wondering the same thing as he leafed through the brochure.

"How do they get all these famous people?" Harry asked.

We were walking along Central Park West in the direction of the Bull Moose Dog Run, which at this early evening hour would be host to the nine-to-five crowd spending what's now known as "quality time" with their pets after the workday.

"I mean why would you bother doing one of these lectures unless you were really desperate for the money yourself?" Harry said as he thumbed through our soon-to-be makeshift Number 2 remover.

"Half of them are over the hill. Tom Le-Body . . . Miranda Roberts . . . Katerina Fatale. Wow! They can really do anything in a photograph. Katerina Fatale must be eighty."

Katerina Fatale, the well-known film star commanded Learning Center readers to "recognize the drama queen within" and "actualize every relationship with a dose of diva power."

My owner came to an abrupt stop. I was

happy we had abandoned the choker collar long ago in my puppyhood.

"I can't believe it," Harry exclaimed. He sat down on a bench and I sidled up next to my owner to see what had taken him by surprise.

Beatrice, Daisy Mae's owner and the supposed owner of the apartment where Overton perished, was a Learning Center speaker. She appeared in the left column of page nineteen opposite a seminar on profiting from real estate foreclosures and another that offered *How to Make Millions Raising Ducks.* The ad read:

Beatrice "Sting Like a Bee" Morris Can You Kwo Bo?

Do you dream of taking would-be attackers down with a combination Double Dragon Banana Fly Kick and an Eastern Wichita Whipsaw? Do you want to learn some of the basics of the mind/body martial art of Kwo Bo, the sensation that is sweeping the nation? Spend an evening with Beatrice "Bee" Morris, the author of Kickboxing Your Way to Health, Wealth and the Body You've Always Dreamed Of. ***The five-time Kwo Bo Platinum Glove Women's Champion***

will take you through all the basic moves and explore the philosophy that makes Kwo Bo the ideal way for any woman (or man) to get in shape and have maximum fun doing it.

Daisy Mae's owner was featured at the top of the page in a flattering photograph, hair streaming in a studio breeze and trim airbrushed body straining in a low-cut karate outfit. Beatrice, it seemed, was some kind of martial arts expert. This came as a surprise to Harry but a greater surprise to me. Why had the "five-time Kwo Bo Platinum Glove Women's Champion" not broken Jackson over her knee when the aging millionaire had seen fit to throw her against a bookcase? According to Marlin, Beatrice hadn't resisted at all, nor seemed capable of resisting. No Eastern Wichita Whipsaw or Double Dragon Banana Fly Kick in sight, unless the moves involved shedding tears and sliding to the floor while your attacker finds the exit.

Nine-to-fivers and their animals packed the Bull Moose Dog Run. Harry and I had to jostle at the gate with three aggressive poodles as substantial as puff pastries. Labradors instinctively loathe this breed. My skin begins to throb as if suffering from a sandpaper rubdown. My breed's earthiness clashes, I suppose, with the poodle's insufferable preciousness. And let us not linger on the recent combination of our breeds into the so-called Labradoodle.

Once we were past the poodles, I felt much better and was about to indulge the olfactories in a snuffle around the trees, but instead of unclipping my leash, Harry held fast. I pulled a bit harder to remind my owner that we were now in the dog run and he could set me free. This did nothing. Looking up, I saw why. Beatrice and Daisy Mae stood on the opposite side of the yard.

"I can't handle her right now," Harry muttered. "Sorry, Randolph. We've got to go."

But Beatrice had already spied my owner.

"Yoohoo, Harry," she said. "Yoohoo."

Harry ignored her. Daisy Mae was in hot pursuit as the outer gate shut behind us, but we had escaped.

"That was close," Harry said.

Shy *Foliage-Finder* though I am, tonight there would be no cover. It was pointless trying to drag Harry into the park nor did I want to take the chance of another encounter with the menacing figure from the night before. I took a deep breath, stopped in the middle of the sidewalk and assumed the position.

"This isn't like you, Randolph," my owner laughed. "Letting everything hang out. Who would think that a snob like you would take the plunge?"

Harry laid the Learning Center brochure on the ground behind me and I looked as disinterested as possible in the gruesome public spectacle occurring aft. My Number 2 scored a direct hit on Katerina Fatale, burying all traces of diva power. Harry dutifully rolled up the Learning Center brochure and deposited it in a trashcan.

Sometimes it takes only a single incident to make a creature realize that something must radically change in his life. Perhaps it was the embarrassment of this moment mixed with my urgent desire to learn more about Overton's death and Imogen's connection to it that made me feel so imprisoned. I had been content to be dependent, to read my books when I could, to be dragged here and there at Harry's whim, but now, I felt a need to push these boundaries. More than mere rebellion — this dog remains loyal no matter what — it was a calling to fulfill something very deep within me. I cared that my owner was easily stung by hopes of Imogen's return, but my concerns for Harry's sensitivities were outweighed by the necessity to discover the truth. We would work through the tears and follow the truth wherever it might lead.

By the time we turned the corner of Ninetieth and walked the seventy-seven steps to the front door of our apartment building, I had resolved to use a supernatural message and then show him Imogen's journal entry. I just hoped that there would be enough Alpha-Bits for what this Labrador had to say.

A Diversion into Dante Spilled Beer Does Damage

I do not, as a rule, have favorites. For example, despite my robust appetite, I have no favorites when it comes to food beyond a distinctly negative attitude toward the tasteless gravel that comes in thirty-pound sacks marked *Fit and Healthy Lo-Cal for Middle-Aged Dogs,* and mercifully gathers dust next to the vacuum cleaner and Harry's disassembled mountain bike in the living room closet. Though I enjoy pastrami, I am equally content with peanut butter and jelly. Though I will gladly eat a porterhouse steak, if I am thrown half a tofu burger I will consider it a welcome nibble.

The same is not true for my literary tastes. My respect for the geniuses who can create whole worlds out of marks on a page knows no bounds. And although I recognize that life often seems one vast gray middle ground of competing likes, I have a clear favorite among the great scribblers: Dante Alighieri, the Florentine poet whose *Inferno* offers me frequent company.

It may seem strange that I disdain spiritualism and the occult, but admire a poet who seems to indulge in the very same nonsense. What is the difference, after all, between Dante trekking through a landscape of broken souls, demons and spirits and Harry and Ivan poking their noses into a dryer in New Jersey in search of a poltergeist?

Much.

Dante is concerned with the ultimate meaning of things. He is concerned with truth. In spite of my commitment to logic and observation, I know that there are some things well beyond our power to comprehend and truths that are not subject to reason and empiricism. I am not merely a slave to my senses. I'm a skeptic out of choice rather than temperament. My senses and my logic are tools, but they are not my only tools. The misled practitioners of medieval medicine followed reason to absurd conclusions and to the detriment of their patients. Before gravity was conceived in theory did this phenomena exist? Of course it did — as did radio waves and DNA. Reason and the senses have their limits.

I believe in love, but I defy anyone to

prove that love exists and I do not mean romantic love, but that other, more generous force idealized as love for one's fellow creatures — what, I believe, the Greeks labeled *agape.* Can anyone prove this kind of love? Where does it dwell? One person can point to the supposed effects of love — an act of charity or self-sacrifice; another person can point to the same results and credit them to selfishness or a pathological hero complex. Yet I believe that love exists and, even more, that it is the foundation of the world. Imogen taught me that love is as real as the olfactory delights of sidewalk paté or Yorkshire pudding — more real even, if that is possible. This is a great mystery and it is a mystery that might never be solved. But animals understand that a great mystery exists. We know it in our bones.

Dante understands that fact as well. He paints a glorious picture of this unknown and makes it come alive as best he can. This endeavor is called Art. Dante never tries to possess the unknown as my ghost hunters do, because he understands that if we are ever to arrive at a solution or even a better understanding, hard work lies ahead — the kind of hard work that can connect the evidence of the senses with the unseen.

Where science may someday go, Art has gone first. I reject the paranormal because it is a shortcut. Ivan and my owner try to pin down the supernatural and make it something they can own, but in doing so they make a mockery of the thing. Harry, at least, had a good excuse. He was trying to regain Imogen.

But I digress. As Dante may have put it: *You and I have gone from bridge to bridge, and spoken of things which my commedia does not mean to sing.*

When we returned home from the Bull Moose Dog Run, Harry sank into the La-Z-Boy recliner that he had inherited from his grandfather Oswald and turned on the television. He opened a beer that he had rescued from the refrigerator and picked up *The Workings of the Spirit Mind.* He had barely finished a page when he threw the book across the room.

"Easier said than done."

The book landed on the basketball hoop that serves as the gateway to Harry's very large clothes hamper beneath. It teetered on the rim then slipped into the net where it got stuck.

"Pathetic. I can't even score."

It was not Harry's finest moment, bathed as he was in the cathode rays of prime time, glassy-eyed and defeated, his left shoe dangling from a toe. His paints and canvases were in their perpetual jumble in my corner of our apartment, but seemed somehow even more jumbled tonight. The only stable thing — always the focal point of comfort for me — was the painting of Imogen's forehead and her green eye peeking out from behind a folded easel.

Harry opened another beer, took a sip and rested it next to the La-Z-Boy. Then, unwisely, he began to rock. The beer bottle tipped and began to gurgle its contents onto the floor. The floors of our old apartment are decidedly uneven and the liquid rushed toward the bookcase. Harry, so engrossed in the happenings on the tube, did not notice and at first I didn't pay much mind either. After all, Harry was always spilling things. But then I remembered Imogen's journal. It was at the base of the bookcase. I hurried over, but I was too late. Beer was pooling around the journal's edges and as I tried to flip it out of the way, the book opened and beer soaked into its pages. Helpless, I watched as my mistress's writings and the code blurred into incomprehensibility.

A Labrador
Soldiers On
But Another Shock
is Delivered

I moved the sopping journal well out of the way so that when (or if) Harry noticed and attempted to clean up the spill, he would not remove this artifact of my mistress to quarters unreachable by Yours Truly.

Afterward, I returned to my corner in a decidedly glummer mood. But not all was lost. Though I would be unable to share the important contents of this last journal entry with Harry, I did remember what the contents were and, most important, had memorized the code — $12CDYZMNBCEFLMIJNOEF8_9$.

Besides, I still had the cereal bridge to my owner. The kitchen table was piled high with Alpha-Bits. But, I recognized, my approach would fail if Harry thought he was getting instructions from Imogen or a schizophrenic rogues gallery of ghosts. I would need a spirit persona, a voice, some character who would help me organize my communications. I decided to call this persona Holmes after Sherlock Holmes. My fondness for the supreme nineteenth-century sleuth was profound and a good name can direct the way we think about something.

Even in better days Harry had been perilously illogical. Holmes would be exceedingly precise but very patient as he led Harry through his thought process. Sir Arthur Conan Doyle's mandate would never be far: *Once you have eliminated the impossible, whatever remains, no matter how improbable, must be the truth.*

Holmes would have to establish ground rules. Harry must not be permitted to reveal the "supernatural" communications to anyone. This was to ensure that Ivan and his kind didn't end up on our doorstep equipped with their paranormal paraphernalia and hopes of finally getting incontrovertible evidence of the world beyond the grave. The next step was to pick a first errand for my owner.

Four people — Iris, Beatrice, the workman and Jackson — had knowledge about Overton's death. All four of these people were related in some way to each other and to Overton. Beatrice was Iris's friend and Iris was Overton's lover. Jackson had known

Overton since prep school, had assaulted Beatrice and had access to the apartment. Iris knew the other three: Beatrice, Jackson and the workman. Harry had access to only two of these people: Beatrice and Jackson. Of these two, Harry was closest to Jackson, but Jackson was the last person that Harry should approach with knowledge of what Marlin had seen.

We were left with Beatrice. She knew both Iris and Jackson. Harry could get to know her. The older woman had seemed very interested in my owner. Could Harry get her to invite him to the apartment? And if he could, what then?

Harry had dozed off and was snoring lightly. Yes, this was going to be more difficult than I had thought. It is one thing to figure out a strategy based on one's observations, sense of smell and suspicions, but quite another to put it into practice when it involves entering strangers' lives and homes. Harry would be doing this on the strength of my messages. But these would only take him so far. He would have to reveal a deep well of his own resources and develop an ability to react appropriately in the moment. On this point, my plan threatened to come undone. I still didn't trust letting this one out on his own.

But I did not need to let this one out on his own I realized. Holmes would inform my owner that I had been "inspired." If I needed to pull Harry in a certain direction, my owner would be instructed to follow.

Ten o'clock, eleven o'clock, midnight — the small digital clock on the microwave blinked in the next day and still Harry slept on in the La-Z-Boy. The late night talk shows yielded to paid infomercials. I did not want to begin my work until Harry had gone into the bedroom for the night, but the night was slipping away. I nuzzled his hand, but he only shifted and fell back asleep.

At two a.m., I took extreme measures: I began to bark.

"Dammit, Randolph, what's wrong?" Harry asked groggily. "I was dreaming about good things. Really good things."

He stared in disbelief at the television. A woman was selling a device that turned steaks into paper-thin strips and transformed old shoelaces into gift-wrapping ribbons.

"What time is it?"

He glanced at the clock on the microwave.

"I'm going to be a wreck tomorrow."

Harry turned off the television and slouched into the bedroom, slamming the door behind him.

I was climbing up onto the chair to begin my work, when his door opened again. I ducked under the table but he did not emerge. A hand reached out from the dark room and fumbled for the living room light switch. The light went off, the hand disappeared and the door shut. I waited a few more minutes and then got to work. There was a full moon and my Labrador eyes lit up the room as if in infrared.

A few hours and one sore nose later, Holmes had completed his first message from the other side:

HARRY THERE IS A MYSTERY AROUND THE DEATH OF OVERTON POSSIBLE FOUL PLAY FOUR PEOPLE INVOLVED ONE IS BEATRICE MY NAME IS HOLMES I AM A SPIRIT WHO WANTS TRUTH TELL NO ONE ABOUT ME OR BAD THINGS WILL HAPPEN FIND BEATRICE GO TO APARTMENT WHERE OVERTON DIED BRING DOG WHERE YOU GO I HAVE INSPIRED HIM FOLLOW HIS LEAD DO THIS SOON DANGER ABOUNDS URGENT DO NOT WRITE A RESPONSE IN LETTERS SPEAK ALOUD

I looked at my work through sleepy eyes. Alpha-Bits is bereft of punctuation and lowercase letters. I hoped it made sense. Now there was only the waiting. I curled in my corner as close to my mistress's image as I could and tried to fall asleep. I glanced around at the peaceful moon-swept space that was our home, and thought about the one member whose absence made it so hard to be at peace. Harry had not dispensed with her clothes. Her towel still hung in the bathroom. Her books still filled the bookcases. But messiness and disorder had gone far to cover up her most delicate touches with the empty takeout cartons, newspapers and randomly discarded boxer shorts and shoes.

Harry stumbled out of the bedroom at eight forty-five the next morning. I expected him to lounge around and perhaps resume reading *The Workings of the Spirit Mind*. Instead he ran about the apartment in a mad rush. As he sped from the bathroom back to his bedroom to get dressed, I put myself in his way. I thought I might be able to nudge him in the direction of my message.

"Move, Randolph," Harry shouted.

My owner pushed me aside and once again disappeared into his bedroom.

"I suppose you want me to take you for a walk? Well, you're out of luck."

He went to the bureau and yanked out the bottom drawer.

"Sometimes I wish you were a cat."

This was a cruel dig, but I was more surprised that Harry had opened the bottom drawer. He hadn't opened the bottom drawer since Imogen had vanished. The drawer contained his formal clothes: pressed oxford shirts, slacks and ties (all folded and arranged once by Imogen). Long before Jackson had begun paying for our rent and food, Harry had done temporary work as a graphic designer. This drawer contained his corporate uniform.

I must have stared.

"That's right, Randolph," Harry said. "I'm going back to work. No more living a life with strings attached."

He slipped into a white shirt.

"If I'm not ready to paint; I'm *not* ready. Final."

He pulled out a tie and snapped it in the air.

"Who says I'll ever be ready?"

Harry struggled with the knot.

"I'm not going to take money on false pretenses. I'm not going to slide along on the dole waiting for something to happen."

I forgot all about my message on the kitchen table. I had an "owner in crisis" and for most of us there is a definite, inborn canine protocol for such situations: provide comfort. If I could have spoken, I would have told Harry that Jackson wouldn't worry if his friend took years to get back to painting. I would have told him that sometimes it is better to wait with patience and even without expectation than to try to fix something by mere action. But I could not speak or force my frozen face into a sign of support or empathy. Instead I sat back on my haunches and raised my two front paws in the air and waved them around.

"Cut it out, Randolph," Harry commanded.

I obeyed. All I could do now was watch him race around the apartment putting on clothes that he hadn't worn in a very long time and fret about how many minutes he had left before he had to walk out the door and get on the subway to Midtown with everyone else who punched a clock.

I stood by the kitchen table and began to bark, hoping that somehow I could direct my owner's attention to my message.

"You keep up the pushiness and I'm sending you to the pound."

Things were going badly, but that, of course, didn't prevent them from getting far worse.

"I'm not walking you this morning, by the way. Ivan is," my owner revealed.

Harry took the milk out of the refrigerator, grabbed a bowl from the sink and headed to the table. *Now we're back on track,* I thought. Harry would see the message, recognize a supernatural hand and be captured by Holmes's words. He would give up all notions of temporary employment, resume a civil posture toward his dog and together we would begin the real work of detection.

Instead with one cavalier sweep of his arm, Harry sent the letters of my message spilling all over the floor, destroying all my hard work.

"Breakfast," he said, pointing at the mess beneath the kitchen table.

He scooped up a handful of Alpha-Bits from the pile that remained in the center of the table, dropped them into his bowl with a splash of milk and began to eat. When he was done, he dropped the bowl in the sink and put on his jacket.

I must have looked extremely forlorn.

"I'm sorry, Randolph. You didn't deserve that. I'll set you up with some steak tonight."

Then my owner was gone. I ate the remnants of my message under the kitchen table and went back to my corner. Then I fell asleep with nothing to show for a very long night.

Ivan arrived at ten, red-faced and out of breath from climbing the stairs.

"What a mess," Ivan said as he surveyed the apartment — an observation that did not deter him from taking a peek into the refrigerator.

"Disgusting," he declared.

Ivan slammed the door shut. He found the leash and snapped it to my collar. When we reached the street, Ivan indicated a spot between a mound of garbage and the flower-bed.

"Do your thing."

Ivan's lavender Mini was illegally parked and idling at the curb. Mr. Apples, his face smeared with chocolate and donut crumbs, pecked at the window and trembled manically. The bird had raided Ivan's breakfast. A rainbow lorikeet on a sugar high is a dangerous creature; a fact Ivan would soon discover when he returned to his vehicle. But I had other worries. Sidewalk traffic was heavy, respectable and well groomed. Every ounce of my *Foliage-Finder* nature was horrified. I looked up at Ivan in silent pleading. He pointed at the spot and tapped his foot. This was truly dismal.

But the walk wasn't without some reward. As we approached our building, Ivan received a phone call.

"Sure I can see you, Beatrice," Ivan said. "Just tell me when and where."

He snapped his cell phone shut. He smelled worried as if he had just received some news that he hadn't been expecting. Then he returned me to the apartment.

I spent the rest of the day recomposing the message to Harry. Sore though my nose was from pushing cereal, I decided to add a postscript:

GRANT DOG UTMOST PRIVACY WHEN
DOING HIS NUMBERS

Harry Learns to Fetch

A Dog Wags His Tail

I took no chances with Holmes's second message. No stray sweep of my owner's arm would ruin my hard work. At great difficulty, I had relocated Harry's bedside lamp to the kitchen table and positioned it so that the message was bathed in its glow. There were no other lights on in the apartment and as night settled outside the window, the effect was striking. I only hoped that my owner would arrive home safe, and soon.

Then I heard his footsteps on the stairs and the front door opened. Harry stood silhouetted against the faint hall light. My owner was good to his word. We would eat well that night. He had returned home with two steaks from Fairway and a D'Aiuto Baby Watson cheesecake.

"What's this?" Harry said, spying the message instantly.

Harry closed the door behind him and

walked straight toward the kitchen table. The cheesecake box, wrapped in red and white baker's string, dangled from an index finger. He swung it back and forth as he read and reread the message.

"Ivan?"

I emitted what to his ears must have sounded like a strangled, sickly bark, but which to mine was a most undignified expletive that I will not reprint here. How could I have been so stupid not to take Ivan's visit into consideration? Of course my owner would attribute the message to the ghost-hunting stooge who had access to our apartment that morning.

Harry called Ivan.

"You almost got me . . . I know you're busy . . . I mean about the message . . . Come on . . . The message . . . What message? . . . The message on the table . . . The kitchen table . . . Really? . . . It wasn't you? . . . The message made out of cereal . . . The P.S. about Randolph needing privacy . . . I forgot I must have told you about the message from the other day . . . I didn't . . . Too weird . . . You and I must be on the same wavelength about this stuff . . . Right . . . Good luck . . ."

Harry put the phone back in its cradle. He wore an amused expression, but I smelled deep puzzlement and the onset of a kind of wild hope. My owner returned to the table and stared at the message. I was on the brink of slipping into a very black mood. Of course, if he didn't believe it or didn't understand, I could repeat the performance that night when no one was about, but the trick was wearing thin.

"Wait a minute," Harry exclaimed. "Even if I did tell Ivan about the cereal message, I definitely didn't tell him about Beatrice. Ivan would have no way of knowing about Beatrice. No way at all."

I gave a loud bark at these words and sauntered to his side. I have never been one to rush.

Harry read from the message. "Bring dog where you go I have inspired him. Follow his lead."

I barked.

"Is that right, Randolph? You're inspired?" Harry asked, patting my head.

I answered again and felt like one of those shameless television dogs barking affirmations at their owner's every question. *So the burglar used a titanium saw to cut through the multipronged lock, Lassie? Woof! Woof!* I hoped Harry would not go too far down this path.

"Do this soon," Harry read. "Mystery

around the death . . . possible foul play . . . four people . . . tell no one about me or bad things will happen . . ."

Harry sat down hard on the chair.

"Man, have I messed up. Ivan already knows; bad things will happen," Harry muttered.

Harry got back up and stomped around the apartment for a few minutes upset by this early misstep, but after a while he became more circumspect. He fished *The Workings of the Spirit Mind; Why Their Logic Defies Ours (And How to Get Around It)* out of the basketball net and looked up *threats* in the index. What he read brought him relief:

A spirit will often use the threat of shadowy and uncertain harm to draw attention to the importance of the message it is trying to communicate. Seldom does the spirit have the power to act upon these threats. More often than not the threat is the spirit's only way of making the living feel a sense of urgency. Most spirits regret this tactic, but feel they simply have no choice. (See "Poltergeist" for exceptions.)

Harry stopped at the window and looked

down at the courtyard of the adjoining building and then up at the thin sliver of night sky.

"Let's hope it's not a poltergeist." He sighed.

Harry looked at the clock on the microwave and realized that it was well past our normal feeding time.

"We're going to eat like kings tonight, Randolph, and then we're going to think more about these developments."

Harry found a frying pan tucked among the garbage bags and deteriorating cleaning supplies under the sink. He scraped it clean with a scrap of steel wool and soon the apartment was filled with the exquisite smell of meat cooking.

"Why don't we have an appetizer?"

Harry opened up the cheesecake and heaped two hearty dollops on our plates. He put one of the plates down on the floor right beneath my nose. I set to work with zeal and soon was peering up at my owner in a rather obvious bid for seconds. He promptly delivered. Harry had seconds as well. Then we both had thirds and moved on to the steak. Precious moments like these make it quite apparent how the males of a species can quickly slip into barbarism without the moderating influence of the feminine.

Finally, Harry put his plate down on the floor, stretched out his legs and rested his fingers on the edge of the kitchen table.

"Let's deal with this message."

He had eaten on his lap for fear of disturbing the message and I could tell that the table had now taken on an almost sacred quality.

"Overton died. There is some kind of mystery around his death. The spirit says foul play. Foul play means murder, doesn't it?"

This was a moment when I could either act or remain silent. As I have said, there was a limited degree to which I wanted Harry to think that I understood him. On the other hand, time was of the essence. I barked.

"And Beatrice and three other people are involved?"

I barked again.

"These four people are *definitely* involved?"

I remained silent. How could I make a definitive statement in the absence of watertight facts? And how could I distinguish between the four? Harry picked up on the more general point implied by my silence.

"These four people are *probably* involved

in Overton's death?"

I whimpered.

"And I have to go to the apartment where it all happened?"

This time I barked to emphasize the importance of an on-site investigation.

"And to do this I have to contact Beatrice?"

Another bark.

"Not that woman again," Harry groaned.

But I could see my owner rally himself to the challenge. He stood up and disappeared into the bedroom. A great tumult ensued as mountains of books, clothes, dishes and paranormal accoutrements collapsed before the explorer. A few minutes later my owner emerged with a pair of jeans.

"Here we are," he said.

Harry pulled a powder blue business card from one of the pockets.

"Beatrice 'Sting Like a Bee' Morris," Harry read. "Kwo Bo. Self-defense for single women. Let a renowned expert show you the ropes. Private and group lessons available."

I had been so intent on Daisy Mae that I hadn't noticed Beatrice give my owner her card that evening at the dog run. This made our work much easier. My owner could simply call her up and arrange to see the apartment.

"But what am I going to say?" Harry asked. "I mean, it's going to be pretty weird to drop in out of the blue."

He walked over to Imogen's portrait to commune with the green eye peeking out from behind the back of another canvas. My owner gazed at the image for a long time. If Imogen had actually been there, Harry would have done the talking. He always had something to say to her and she was by nature a listener — her thoughtful eyes registering complete comprehension behind her narrow glasses. But there was no comprehension now and Harry returned to stare at the kitchen table. He trailed a solitary finger through the pile of Alpha-Bits in the center.

"It could be a follow-up to the séance. A spirit investigation, a complementary visit to make certain everything's okay."

I barked for what I instantly swore to myself would be the last time that evening.

Harry smiled down at me as he reached for the phone to call Beatrice.

"This is wild, Randolph. I almost feel like you have a brain . . . that you can understand me."

Wild, indeed, dear Harry, I thought. We were finally underway. If I could have smiled, I would have. Instead, I did something else: I wagged my tail. I rarely do, but as another favorite of Yours Truly, the English poet Auden, remarks and I paraphrase: *At moments of extreme happiness, we all wish we had a tail to wag.*

RANDOLPH REMEMBERS HIS CHILDHOOD A VISIT TO THE SCENE OF THE CRIME

Memory is a fickle thing. Ask ten people at the scene of a traffic accident what each saw and you will get ten different stories. The car was red. No, the car was black. The driver was old. No, the driver was little more than a child. The victim dove in front of the car. No, the victim slipped on a banana peel. This phenomenon is the bane of attorneys and the playground of neuroscientists and all those interested in the workings of the brain. The question is further complicated by emotion. Even those with the best memories should be aware that there is a process that colors what they remember with feelings. It is not simply a question of wanting to remember something a certain way, but of the hidden connections between positive and negative feelings, sometimes long past, that change the way we perceive the present even as it is happening.

I have seldom worried that my own memories are faulty, because I have two distinct advantages over humans. You have likely heard the concept that seven dog years equal one human year. In fact, it's more like ten for the first couple of years of a dog's life and then fewer per year as we age. Alas, whatever the exact conversion, this still means that at my current age of five, I am well on my way toward the middle years. Already on mornings when New York is wrapped in a chill fog, I feel the rheumatoid arthritic pangs to which we Labradors are susceptible. On the other hand, the time that has elapsed since my early childhood is, after all, but a few years, leaving much less time to distort memories.

My nose, though, is my main advantage. The memories of my early years are filled with vivid scenes that I captured with both my snout and eyes and each sense reinforces the other. As I have mentioned, all of this sniffing and seeing has built a catalogue of scents that I can compare against other scents and experiences the longer I live.

Humans do not actually detect much through their noses at all, no matter how fond they are of saying that they can "sniff out trouble" or "smell a rat." A brief example. Before there was Harry, Imogen had another boyfriend. No one could ever match

Harry in Imogen's affections, but this man was accomplished enough to hold my mistress's eye for a time. I never liked him — not even for a minute. I had smelled him out before their third date. Lurking beneath the expensive but overly musky cologne was nervousness and deception. A casual reference by Imogen to a friend's wife, and the smell of his nervousness doubled and the scent of deception became almost unbearable. No break in his smarmy delivery, no dimming of his Panavision smile, no flicker of uncertainty on his face, but beneath this façade my olfactories were capturing a complete breakdown. There were other smells as well: the fresh scent of a child and a delicate female perfume — a perfume nothing like Imogen's. Puppy though I was, I knew a thing or two about life, courtesy of the house-training newspapers that my mistress had laid out in a corner of the kitchen — the newspapers that had taught me how to read. Though a woman of refined tastes, my mistress could not resist the tabloids and as a result my very first reading primer was a *New York Post,* the paper that long ago set the standard for screaming headlines with:

HEADLESS BODY IN TOPLESS BAR.

The gossip columns provided tales of deception and betrayal that shaped my impressionable puppy brain while they taught me the basics of the English language.

I soon concluded that this man was married and had a family. It took Imogen another month to find out the truth for herself and then only at great embarrassment during an office Christmas party that she attended against his advice.

Most people are familiar with those dreams in which danger is very close and yet the dreamer, his limbs as heavy as concrete, cannot escape. Every time I saw this man or heard Imogen speaking with him on the phone, I had the same desperate sense. How could my mistress not sniff out this rat? But, of course, she could not. All the points vulnerable to normal human inspection, his appearance, his voice, et cetera, he had made impervious to scrutiny.

Smell would guide us in the Overton matter as well. No human knew that memory smelled too, even ancient memories — sometimes with the very freshness of the present moment. And no human knew — but I knew — that he could smell of guilt or reek of homicide.

Two days passed before we could see Beatrice and visit the apartment — two days during which I worked almost full-time on the code without any headway. Harry had made an appointment with Beatrice to meet at the apartment in the early afternoon. We took our oft-traveled route to Jackson's suite at the Belvedere, passing the brownstone apartment that had caused my owner such sadness on Christmas Day. No fire glowed in the hearth now, the windows were dark and the Christmas tree had already been deposited on the curb for garbage pickup.

Of course, instead of turning into the Belvedere's lobby to visit Jackson, we crossed the street and approached a large prewar building with an exquisite Art Deco canopy of glass and steel. To Harry's surprise, Beatrice waited for us beneath the canopy instead of in her apartment. Daisy Mae was nowhere to be seen. Both facts were in keeping with Marlin's observations that neither Beatrice nor her dog were occupants of the apartment and thus of little surprise to me. However, I also happened to notice Beatrice watching what I thought was Ivan's lavender Mini speeding away from her building just moments before we arrived.

"I needed some fresh air," Beatrice explained in response to my owner's quizzical expression. Then she promptly turned the attention back to him.

"Aren't you looking spectacular?" Beatrice said. Smells from our first encounter mingled in a cloud of Chanel No. 5 and her own natural scent. Anxiety, suspicion, anger, temper, dishonesty and potential violence were all present, but very much diminished. Beatrice's deep dislike of males seemed to have been overwhelmed by her attraction to my owner.

"Very spectacular," Beatrice emphasized.

Harry blushed. Not only was Beatrice his mother's age, she bore a faint resemblance to the Midwestern matriarch.

"And you look very healthy," my owner said.

"Healthy. How adorable," Beatrice laughed.

She whisked us through the lobby, winking at the doorman who made no attempt to open the door for her.

"Such a strange thing to have a man die in one's home," Beatrice said as the elevator doors closed.

"Then again I suppose dozens of people have died in my space over the hundred or so years this building's been standing."

"Good point," Harry said, taking the opportunity to reference the paranormal. "But the dozens of other ghosts are probably not there. A recent death like Overton's should make him the standout spirit in the space. The fact that there are living who knew him and, more important, knew how he died — the violence of it — that will tend to keep him prominent."

"What violence?" Beatrice asked. "He had a heart attack. Millions of people have heart attacks."

Even a bucket of Chanel No. 5 would not have drowned the powerful stench of anxiety and desperation that Beatrice shed as she spoke these words.

"Millions of people might have heart attacks," Harry said, "but millions of people don't die suddenly on the bathroom floor of somebody else's apartment in a pool of their own urine."

A bell rang and the doors of the elevator slid open. Beatrice grabbed hold of Harry's arm and led us to the apartment.

The layout was familiar from my observations on Christmas Day, but the smells transfixed me. Every interior space has its primary scent. Even human beings know this much. A strange home has a scent which a visitor can smell plainly but which the occupant cannot. This smell is usually composed of two things: (1) the distinct physical scent of the chief inhabitants and (2) the kind of food they cook. But the smell of this apartment was not ordinary. It was the smell of transitory habits and vagabond bodies. It most certainly did not bear the smell of Daisy Mae thus further confirming Marlin's observations, although there was a prominent female smell that I suspected was that of Iris and a less prominent female smell that was likely Beatrice's. The smells carried a cast of characters and bore a kaleidoscopic range of human emotion: excitement and joy; despair and hate; the bitterness of death and the hope of birth. And this was just in the entranceway.

"You know I think all this ghost stuff is nonsense, but if it floats your boat, it floats mine," Beatrice said from the kitchen. "Want a drink? I'm fixing myself a champagne cocktail."

"No thanks," Harry said.

My owner approached the long walnut table that dominated the living room/dining room.

"Why not? It's almost New Year's Eve. The whole world wants to party."

"No thanks, really," Harry said.

He plugged a cord into the back of his equipment and flipped on the power. The machine made a terrible screech and then fell silent.

"What's that thing?" Beatrice asked, sipping from a crystal flute.

"It's a spectrometer," Harry said. The "spectrometer" was, in fact, a multipurpose battery recharger brought along by my owner for show. Like the La-Z-Boy, it had been inherited from Grandfather Oswald who had used it to jump his John Deere lawn tractor on the rare occasions the machine failed to start.

"Impressive," Beatrice said. "What does it do?"

"Measures electrical fields that correlate to spectral presence."

Beatrice looked confused.

"In lay terms," Harry explained, "it finds spirits."

"Any spirits yet?"

"Nope."

A little while later Harry asked if he could see the rest of the apartment.

"Don't you want to bring that thing with you?" Beatrice asked as they left the living room/dining room.

"No. It's collecting data."

"Rightio."

Beatrice swanned down the hallway.

The distance from the living room/dining room where the séance took place to the bathroom where Overton died was greater than I had expected. It struck me that some of Overton's initial sounds could have gone unheard by the group gathered around Madame Sosostris.

The bathroom was a renovated space done along post-modern lines. Every implement, the tub, the sink and the toilet, was made of stainless steel. The towels and the toilet paper had not been changed since Overton's death. They reeked of one powerful thing: agony. Someone, Overton I imagined, had been in severe pain in that space.

"Violent," Harry said.

He stood in the doorway behind Beatrice. "What's that?"

"He was in pain," Harry said. Harry had never mentioned pain before.

"He was in pain? I thought he died right away," asked Beatrice. I could smell the return of her anxiety despite the calming influence of the alcohol she had just consumed.

"I didn't remember it until I stood here again, but he was holding his crotch . . ."

"The autopsy said heart. Maybe it was unrelated. Maybe he had a herpes outbreak and a heart attack at the same time. Maybe the pain from the herpes brought on the heart attack. Who knows? Who really cares?

I've said it before and I'll say it again. The man was a bastard."

Harry wasn't listening. He stared into space, remembering.

"It was terrible actually. I can see his face. It was contorted and red and he was holding on to his crotch like there was a gunshot wound."

Beatrice returned to the kitchen and poured herself another champagne cocktail.

"You sure you don't want one? In my hands they're out of this world. In my hands lots of things are out of this world."

I snuffled around the base of the toilet. Someone had done a thorough mopping and I could smell nothing but lemon and bleach. I worked my way around to the back. The wall behind the toilet featured a little door that I supposed gave access to the pipes. I froze. From behind this door I smelled the distinctive odor of burnt plastic. I nuzzled the door. Harry took notice.

"Follow his lead," my owner muttered, reciting the instructions from the cereal message.

"What's that?" Beatrice called from the kitchen.

Harry opened the door and I introduced my snout into the tiny space. The smell of burnt plastic was stronger, but there was no evidence of what had made the smell. There was nothing there but metal pipes and a shut-off valve. I backed up and Harry closed the door. We returned to the living room/dining room.

"Find what you wanted?" Beatrice asked.

"Not even close."

"Do we have a disgruntled literary spirit in residence or has he flown to some hell for bad writers and even worse human beings?"

"No comment," Harry said. He pretended to interpret the meter on the battery recharger.

"This device has no opinion on his fate," he announced.

Harry unplugged Grandfather Oswald's machine and wrapped up the cord.

"You know, I loved him once too," Beatrice said. She had moved on to her third champagne cocktail.

"Overton?"

Beatrice nodded.

"Really?"

"It was a long time ago. Before his wife . . . before Iris . . . when he was pure."

I drew close to Beatrice and inhaled. No change of scent. No emotion. She seemed to be fabricating the relationship.

"I don't mean pure in any angelic sense. I

mean pure in that literary way — before he became a hack and a fixture of the New York culture circuit. He left me."

"I'm sorry."

"Don't be. Nothing ventured; nothing lost."

Beatrice drew near my owner.

"Give Bee a kiss," she breathed lustily, putting her champagne cocktail down on the counter with a loud clink and approaching my owner.

Harry dropped the cord to Grandfather Oswald's battery charger with a clatter.

"For the New Year," Beatrice insisted.

"I'd better go," Harry said.

"But you just arrived," Beatrice said. "You have wonderful eyes. Do you know that? I'd call them *absentminded luminous.*"

Urgent action was required. I jogged to the door and began to scratch and whine.

"What's wrong with that dog?" Beatrice asked.

"I really have to go," Harry insisted, extricating himself from the grip of the Kwo Bo expert and her dangling champagne cocktail.

"Don't go," Beatrice pled.

"My dog," Harry stammered. "He has bladder control problems. Sorry."

Harry and I raced to the elevator, which

was mercifully quick to arrive.

Beatrice called after us as the doors slid shut. "You can come by anytime, beautiful, but next time leave the dog at home."

A Dog Has a Breakthrough But Must Keep it to Himself

"I have no idea what the point of that was." Harry sighed and retreated to the La-Z-Boy when we arrived back home. He had bought a *New York Post* on the way but tossed it onto the floor without giving it a look. Soon he was engrossed in television and I began to peruse the tabloid.

The huge two-word headline caught my attention immediately:

HOT DOG

Below the words a dachshund with toasted fur and charred whiskers stared pathetically out at the reader. I nosed my way to the article on page three and learned that a virtual epidemic of dog electrocutions was plaguing Manhattan.

Male dogs, who had a penchant for lifting their legs and marking street objects with their urine, had recently been suffering electrocution. All around town protective covers were coming off the bases of lamp-posts through vandalism, neglect or badly driven snowplows. Whatever the reason, live wires were being exposed. Normally this wouldn't be very dangerous, but when contacted by the steady stream of a Number 1, the wires became deadly. Two hundred and forty volts of electricity would travel up the conductor-rich liquid, through the dog's delicate delivery system and tear through the canine's body like a band of angry Visigoths.

Few dogs survived. The ones who did were severely damaged goods.

An Alsatian in Harlem had lost all of his hair and tap-danced off the sidewalk into oncoming traffic. One sheltie on Fourteenth Street had actually exploded. Dog lovers were outraged. The *Post* fanned the controversy by reporting that the Kennel Club of Greater New York was planning a so-called die in at city hall despite the mayor's vow to arrest all guilty of trespassing. The newspaper, upholding a tabloid tradition, ended on a lachrymose note: " 'Gary was just a peace-loving Pekingese,' one distraught dog owner moaned. 'I know he's in doggy heaven right now just wishing he was here to comfort me.' "

My first reaction to the news of these electrocutions was selfish. How many times would I have done just the same against the base of a streetlamp but for the restraint of my *Foliage-Finder* nature? But then I remembered the smell of burnt wires at the scene of Overton's demise and the bathroom made almost entirely out of stainless steel . . .

Eureka!

I had solved the mechanics of Overton's death.

The recent electrification of Number 1s was not limited to the world of dogs. It had happened to a famous writer in an apartment on the Upper West Side.

During the car ride back from our ghost-hunting expedition to New Jersey, Harry had mentioned Overton's last word: *Elektra.* My owner, or rather Ivan's overexcited analysis, had gotten it wrong.

Overton had not been referring to a figure from Greek myth or the Freudian follow-up. He was trying to form the word *electricity* or perhaps *electrocuted.* He was trying to express the "how" of his own sudden death.

The voltage had not been as severe as the street occurrences (or else the autopsy would have revealed it), but it had been sufficient to end the life of a man — if that man was wearing a pacemaker.

Harry remained stationed in the La-Z-Boy until the wee hours. Unfortunately, I would be keeping this revelation to myself for now, because while I waited for my owner to depart the living room I fell into a deep and dream-filled sleep from which I didn't awaken until late the next morning with a sharp nudge from my owner.

A Day at the Spa
New Year's Eve
Reflections for
Dog and Man

Harry had delivered the sharp nudge because he had decided that New Year's Eve was the perfect day to redeem the golden ticket, Jackson's Christmas present to Yours Truly. Accordingly, by eleven-fifteen that morning, I found myself in a swimming pool at the Pooch Palace — Canine Pool and Spa in Midtown Manhattan next to Bam Bam, a rottweiler with a particularly enormous skull and troubling incisors. Luckily, Bam Bam was a pleasure to talk to — one of the few dogs I have met who could actually focus. He had *Squat-and-Drop* written all over him, but possessed many *Foliage-Finder* sensibilities.

Bam Bam and I remained in the shallow end comparing notes on the relations between species.

"If we were slaves, we would do things for *them*," the rottweiler said. "As it is, they do things for *us*. I don't walk her; she walks me. I don't feed her; she feeds me. The list goes on and on. Can you imagine anything more humiliating than scurrying around after humans with a plastic bag to pick up their feces? It's bad enough having their eyes all over us when we do our numbers."

"Yet to be fed is to be fed on *their* time and to be walked is to be walked where *they* want to go."

"Not if I'm at the end of the leash, brother," Bam Bam countered. "I always do the driving."

"Every wise man is a free man and every fool a slave," I replied, turning to the great Roman orator and statesman for this chestnut on the question of freedom and the will.

"Uh oh, someone's been nipping at the quote book," Bam Bam said.

"Cicero is something of a soul mate to me," I explained.

"Well, I bet Cicero never curled up for a nap on a sunny spot in a living room or had a good roll in sidewalk paté," Bam Bam said.

"Ah, sidewalk paté . . ." I sighed and drifted away to Elysium.

Discussion of my vice can wait no longer. Sidewalk paté is every dog's vice really. Although country dogs lack the sidewalks of their city brethren, there is no shortage of the paté. You likely already know what sidewalk paté is even if you haven't heard the term. It is the most wretched biological refuse one can find smeared among the grit and divots of the pavement and beckoning for a roll. When an immaculately groomed Collie, for example, suddenly flips onto his back and wriggles in complete delight — you can be sure that he is rolling in paté. The paté can be the remains of a mouse, a chicken bone or a three-day-old milkshake spill, whatever it is, the material must be fetid and decomposing. In short, a revolting patch of rot.

On a physical level, dead and rotting things simply smell delicious to a dog's nose. Sidewalk paté is so delicious that a dog just wants to wrap himself in the smells like they were silk sheets and smear them into his coat for extended review. Biologists have claimed that the behavior is a way for us to mask our scents from predators — a dismal speculation by those who lack the imagination to comprehend our magnificent noses.

You probably have dismissed the behavior as mere dog play, but if it is play, it is the most serious of play — one might even call it deep play. On a philosophical level, the behavior connects a dog to the universe — to the joy of being a dog. And the joy of being a dog is the joy of a life that does not fear the reality of life's opposite: death and its rich olfactory layers of decay.

Although dead and rotting things may be found in abundance on the streets of New York, it is not every dead or rotting thing that appeals to me. Sidewalk paté, like any delicacy, must have just the right quantities of odors to bewitch, but when it does bewitch me, nothing has ever stolen my reason or stilled my every action like it. Sherlock Holmes had his cocaine; I have my sidewalk paté.

"You all there, fellah?" Bam Bam asked me.

"There is *nothing* like sidewalk paté," I observed.

"Nothing," Bam Bam agreed.

A respectful silence followed broken only by a Chihuahua thrashing for its life in the deep end.

"What are canine waterobics anyway?" I asked, reading the schedule of pool activities on the wall.

"They take the fatties, throw 'em in the drink and don't let 'em out until they've gotten fit or drowned," said Bam Bam.

The wetsuit-clad attendant scooped the Chihuahua from the pool after it had gone under for the fourth time.

We had edged into deeper water, but Bam Bam hesitated to go farther than his shoulders. His muscle-to-fat ratio did not make him buoyant. Yours Truly, on the other hand, bobbed about like an inflatable pool toy.

"What are you in for?" I asked.

"The three-year-old decided to play horsy on big doggy and big doggy was injured," Bam Bam said. "My herniated disc is costing her a fortune. Is that one yours?"

Bam Bam pointed his nose in the direction of my owner. Harry sat in a corner of the pool deck reading the newspaper.

"Looks very sad," Bam Bam said.

"He is very sad."

"Seems like a nice enough guy."

"Too nice."

"A pushover?"

"All too often."

"That's good for you."

"Not really. He's adrift."

"They're all adrift in one way or another. There'd be total chaos if I wasn't the one in charge of mine."

"Which one is yours?"

"The scrawny dye-job on the cell phone. Middle of a divorce. New boyfriend's not calling back. There's a sale on at Saks. Oh the drama," Bam Bam said.

Harry put the newspaper down, stood up and stretched. Bam Bam's owner hung up her phone and tried to make polite conversation with him.

"Those two seem to get along swimmingly, hah hah," Bam Bam's dye-job remarked.

"Right," Harry said.

"We should have a playdate."

Harry did not respond.

"I mean our dogs should have a playdate, hah hah." The dye-job blushed. "Not you and me."

"Oh."

"Where do you live?"

"Upper West Side."

"Oh my God. So do we. Do you go to the dog run at the Natural History Museum?"

"Bull Moose?"

"Exactly."

"Sometimes."

"I should definitely get your number."

I began to flounder desperately in the pool. Once again I would take one for the team.

"Is your dog alright?"

"I'm not sure."

The attendant heaved me out of the water and onto the pool deck. Harry toweled me down.

"See you around," Bam Bam said.

"I hope so. You're very articulate."

"Thanks. The ex subscribed to *The Economist.*"

Bam Bam's owner had followed Harry over to the side of the pool.

"Maybe we'll see each other at the dog run?"

"Maybe."

Harry snapped on my leash and led the way up a flight of cramped stairs to the street. It was good to be out in the winter air.

"Some women," Harry muttered.

We walked east to Eighth Avenue.

"Did you like your first swim?"

I wagged my tail.

"At least you got some exercise."

I stopped wagging my tail at the word *exercise*.

We had walked the forty blocks to the Pooch Palace — Canine Pool and Spa and we would have to walk another forty home. Taxis, subways and buses forbid large dogs (smaller canines, though, travel freely about the city on all forms of transportation in their carriers). In New York there is an exclusive service called Animal Taxi that could accommodate the heftier dog, but it was too dear for my owner's wallet.

It was late afternoon on New Year's Eve and the police were assembling for crowd control. Barricades had been erected to channel the hundreds of thousands of people expected to watch the ball drop at midnight. Already tourists and partygoers streamed south toward Times Square. We reached Columbus Circle and followed Central Park West home against the crowd.

"It's just you and me tonight, Randolph. I'll uncork the bubbly."

Harry struck that glum, self-consciously cheerful note that people use at such dismal moments — as if there was an audience just offscreen that could identify perfectly with the speaker's plight.

Needless to say, no champagne emerged upon arrival home. Instead, Harry ordered Chinese and we shared pan-fried dumplings, spareribs and soy sauce chicken. Then he settled down in the La-Z-Boy to watch a three-hour repeat of *The World's Greatest Natural Disasters*.

Yours Truly curled up in his corner as midnight and the New Year approached. I returned once again to the code. *12CDYZM-NBCEFLMIJNOEF8$_9$*. Using the physician's adage for diagnosis of disease (when you hear hoofbeats think horses not zebras), I started with the obvious, a simple substitution cipher. For any solver of newspaper cryptograms or puzzle books, the idea should be familiar. E, T, N, A, O, R, I, S and H are the nine most frequent letters in English. The least frequent are J, K, Q, X and Z. However, letter frequencies can only be truly helpful when the message to be deciphered is long, which my mistress's was not. Moreover, Imogen had removed the so-called word boundaries — all the words of the message ran together, adding another layer of solving difficulty. I moved on to the Gronsfeld Cipher, a system in which a number is used as the key to break a code, and got stuck there. Even though Imogen had underlined the Gronsfeld passage in her cryptography book, my efforts only led to a throbbing headache and the nonsense words *spinach cloud.*

Connecting all of this to Imogen would have to come later. I had the "how" of Overton's death and the next step was to convey my latest revelations to Harry as soon as possible before whatever was out there waiting for my owner grew impatient and came after him.

The phone rang. Harry didn't budge from the La-Z-Boy. The machine picked up.

"Leave a message after the beep," Imogen's voice said before trailing off into an uncertain whisper. "Harry, is it a beep?"

A digital beep was followed by the sound of revelers.

"Happy New Year, Harry. This is Ely, buddy. You're probably out, but if you get this, the crew is at the Dive Room and we'd love to see you. Okay, bud . . . that's it for now . . . have a good one . . ."

Ely was lost to the raucous human sea that was once my owner's favorite East Village bar. Harry had always been very popular. Before Imogen he had been the model New York bachelor. With Imogen he had been the model male component of the model New York couple.

The World's Greatest Natural Disasters was entering its third and final tormented hour. Harry watched as an animated Krakatoa exploded sending clouds of ash miles into the sky. A little while later Germany was pummeled by hailstones the size of grapefruits. Then it was time for the New Year's ball to drop. Harry changed the channel to find the event.

"Randolph," Harry instructed, "say good-bye to the old year."

I looked up at my owner. He was leaning forward in Grandfather Oswald's La-Z-Boy with the remote control and a beer. I sidled up to him. No one should be so alone.

"What the hell am I doing talking to a dog about the New Year? Dogs have no concept of time."

No concept of time, indeed. The average Labrador lives scarcely more than a decade and so each new calendar year is heavy with significance. It seems that the weight of all that has happened since the beginning of the world is upon me at moments like this.

The announcer began the countdown to midnight.

Ten . . . Nine . . . The television cameras panned the crowd that filled Times Square. A girl with curly hair blew a streamer into the ear of a boy wearing a college sweatshirt; strobe lights broke people's faces into silver shards; the digital tickers ran in endless loops up and down and around buildings carrying the news; and everyone — moving, laughing, screaming, shouting, waving, the rare still and serious face in the crowd — looked so very contemporary and simultaneously so very time bound, each one as much a period piece as the people in the famous photograph of the sailor kissing the woman at the end of World War II. *Eight . . . Seven . . .* One did not know what the future would look like, but whatever came, the present would eventually be locked away somewhere in a glass museum case. *Six . . .*

Then I thought of Overton dead only nine days — that unknown quantity of a man who was murdered with his fly open — and Marlin, my nervous Guatemalan tree sloth. And I thought of Jackson and Harry and finally Imogen — how I missed her intelligence and her kindness. And I thought of how it was possible that I had not really known her at all — did not know any of them at all really. But I was at least going to try to find out. The work that we do might not matter a jot. We might be fools for even trying. Then, again, maybe the exact opposite is true and we are suited for nothing so well as the time in which we live and meant for nothing but its challenges and its loves. *Five* . . .

A piece of verse came to mind. It was not the work of my beloved Dante but of a more recent genius: W. H. Auden, the British poet who had called my narrow island home for several decades. He too had faced a New Year filled with doubt and dark musings — the New Year 1940 when a great war loomed over the world. *Four* . . . His words now flowed through my mind, a sad and graceful music:

The situation of our time
Surrounds us like a baffling crime.

There lies the body half-undressed

We all had reason to detest,
And all are suspects and involved
Until the mystery is solved

Three . . .

And under lock and key the cause
That makes a nonsense of our laws.
O Who is trying to shield Whom?
Who left a hairpin in the room?
Who was the distant figure seen
Behaving oddly on the green?

Two . . . Harry lifted his empty beer in a toast to the screen.

Why did the watchdog never bark?
Why did the footsteps leave no mark?
Where were the servants at that hour?
How did a snake get in the tower?

One . . . The Waterford Crystal ball hit bottom. The crowd drowned the stillness of our tiny apartment.
The New Year had begun.

Harry Plays Fetch with Beatrice Again

A Dog Meets a Woman without a Scent

The second message from Holmes appeared within a few hours, on New Year's Day. Harry had wandered off to bed soon after midnight and I was once again left in the dark with the Alpha-Bits. The pile of cereal had become a permanent fixture on the kitchen table and the first message remained untouched for reference. I cleared a new place beside it and began the process of finding and dragging each letter into place with my nose. A wet nose might be evidence of a healthy dog, but it is a serious obstacle to cereal work. For each letter I placed, two disintegrated into a yeasty paste on my nose. Long after the noise of our champagne-addled neighbors stumbling home up the stairs gave way to predawn silence, I struggled. The inelegant result arrived at sunrise:

OVERTON ELECTROCUTED BY DEVICE
IN
BATHROOM
DEVICE NO LONGER IN APARTMENT
MEET WITH BEATRICE IMMEDIATELY AT
APARTMENT ASK HER TO
BRING IRIS
ARRANGE TO SEE JACKSON SOON HE
COULD BE
INVOLVED SOMEHOW
BUT LET HIM DO THE TALKING
OBEY DOGS LEAD AT ALL TIMES YOU
MIGHT BE
BEING FOLLOWED

Harry emerged from his bedroom at ten. Seeing the message on the table he slid into a chair and put his chin in his hands. Soon he was utterly engrossed.

"Electrocuted," Harry gasped. "And Jackson involved? This is serious."

Five minutes later, Harry had Jackson on the phone. The earliest they could meet was two days hence on January 3. Jackson seemed to be in a hurry and cut the phone call short. Then Harry reached Beatrice. He convinced her that Iris must be present for what he called a "spectral narrative follow-up." A meeting was arranged for that day.

This time Harry was instructed to go

directly to the apartment. The elevator gave a ring as usual when we arrived at their floor and the door of the apartment promptly opened. Beatrice greeted us from the entrance and then introduced us to Iris in the short narrow hallway that led to the living room.

Iris was nothing like I had expected. She looked to be Beatrice's age, but other similarities were scarce. Where Beatrice was hard and outgoing, Iris was soft and distinctly private. She barely met Harry's eyes when he reintroduced himself. Instead of the near constant anxiety of which Beatrice reeked, Iris offered nothing more to the olfactories than a bland, indifferent scent. When Iris spoke she reminded me of how Vivien Leigh played Blanche Dubois in *A Streetcar Named Desire*.

"Oh my," she said. "This *is* a tight squeeze. How I *do* hate tight squeezes."

My owner nodded.

"Happy New Year," Harry said. Iris ignored him.

"And is he alright in tight spaces, the poor thing?" she asked, gesturing down at me.

There was something strangely disconnected in Iris's voice. Her sentences began almost randomly and ended with a sigh.

Beatrice rolled her eyes and tapped her fingers on her leg impatiently.

"Happy New Year, doll," Beatrice said, scanning my owner provocatively from head to foot and asking, "Where's your equipment?"

"Equipment?"

Then Harry remembered Grandfather Oswald's battery recharger.

"You mean the spectrometer?"

"Perhaps," Beatrice purred.

"I don't need it today. Today we're doing the spectral narrative — pen and paper work."

"Spectral what?" Beatrice asked. She shuffled into the kitchen to fix a drink for herself.

"Stories," Iris said. "I do believe the dear means stories. Stories about ghosts."

"I want to learn more about how you perceived Overton the living person," Harry said. "And how you perceive Overton the dead person."

"How I do adore sherry," Iris said. Her bland, indifferent smell did not change at the mention of Overton.

"No sherry for you," Beatrice said. "It mixes with your medication."

"My medication," Iris said and ran her finger along the windowsill like a woman in a trance.

"Perhaps the young man might fancy a glass," Iris said.

"Would the young man *fancy* a glass?" Beatrice asked Harry.

My owner had brought a notebook along as a prop and now posed with his ballpoint pen at the ready.

"No thank you," Harry said. "Maybe we should start with your perceptions of Overton the living person."

"Troubled angel." Iris sighed. "Little boy."

"Oh Lord, spare me the pity," Beatrice said.

"Love, not pity," Iris insisted without sounding insistent.

Iris remained at the window looking out across the space at the building opposite. Her eyes danced from window to window and briefly settled on Jackson's home. Marlin had taken up temporary residence on the second limb from the top of the ficus and was chewing on a leaf. It had been a week since I had seen him. I was glad that the Guatemalan tree sloth remained intact and wondered what more he might have to report.

"Where to begin?" Beatrice asked.

She had ducked into the kitchen and was pouring herself another drink. She leaned her elbows on the counter and took a sip of sherry.

"He was your standard cad really. He made promises that he never intended to keep. He used people and threw them away. If someone caught his eye — and I mean anyone because he was omnivorous, woman *or* man — they would be the flavor of the month and then when he was bored . . . *ta ta* and thanks for the memories."

Beatrice finished the sherry in one long sip and pushed back off her elbows.

"What good is salt if it has lost its taste?" Iris said, waving her hand dismissively, and then seemed to sink back into her own thoughts.

"Were you one of those people?" Harry asked Beatrice.

"Oh no," Beatrice said. "My little drama happened long before Dorian Gray became Dorian Gray. I said that he was pure then and I meant it. He was different long ago. He didn't know how to take and not give back. He learned that later."

She leaned over Harry and her voice dropped to a whisper. "Iris is the wreckage."

Iris hadn't moved from her spot at the window. Her finger continued to trace a pattern in the dust on the ledge.

"She let him take too much."

"How can someone who has such a reputation for being one way actually be the exact opposite?" Harry asked.

"What sweet naiveté," Beatrice exclaimed. "There's no greater divide than the people who are in a circle and the people who are outside of it. Everyone in the circle knew the truth about Overton. Everyone knew that he was a letch who wrote stories that always managed to get around to the topic of his dead wife. But nobody would ever say anything against him publicly. He had the ability to make or break reputations. Besides he had that literary authority that descends on some writers whether they deserve it or not."

Beatrice lit a cigarette and tossed her hair, for a moment reminding me of a black-and-white movie actress.

"Overton was a force of nature," she concluded. "He crushed people, especially women."

Iris awoke from her trance to request a cigarette.

"How I adore cigarettes," she said. "I'm quite sure it will be perfectly fine with my medication."

"I'm quite sure it *won't* be perfectly fine with the medication, but have one anyway, babe," Beatrice said. She handed her friend a cigarette and lit it. Iris returned to the window.

"Paris." Iris sighed. "Cigarettes remind me of Paris. How I adore Paris."

"He filled them with hopes," Beatrice said, sitting down at the table next to Harry.

"Hopes?" Harry asked.

"Not just the hopes that lovers have, not, you know, the usual hopes of staying together or being the only one for that person and so on. No, I mean diabolical hopes. The kind of hopes that make a little person think that they're a big person and a stupid person think that they're a smart person. Lyell made people think better of themselves, but not in a good way, not in a way that could last."

Beatrice looked over at Iris.

"He left a few suicides in his wake."

"Is she going to be one of them?" Harry asked.

"Not if I can help it," Beatrice said. "She's on a ton of medication. I'm surprised she's still breathing. I'm not quite sure what Iris is taking, but she's far away from planet earth. There's a good man who loves her like any woman would want to be loved. He's loved her for years. He'll never stop, but she just isn't interested — not at all."

Beatrice put her hand on my owner's arm.

"I have a confession to make," she said. Harry tensed.

"My confession is: Iris owns this apartment. She lives here. I'm the one who lives in the dump in the eighties."

"Why did you lie?" Harry asked.

"I lied because I felt small. I came to the séance that night to tell Overton off and scare him away from my friend. I left before he arrived because I lost my nerve. He was one of those people who never seem wrong in person no matter how wrong they actually are."

"So this is Iris's apartment?" Harry asked. He looked over at the woman by the window. She had smoked her cigarette down to her knuckles.

"All hers," Beatrice said.

Iris finally noticed the state of her cigarette and snuffed it out on the windowsill.

"The man who loves her pays for it. He has for the longest time."

The windowsill was one of those generous prewar expanses as wide as a table and Iris had climbed onto it. She sat next to the window, which was open slightly to combat the staleness of the overheated apartment.

"You really don't worry about her?"

"Jumping?" Beatrice asked. "God no.

She's too much of a lady."

I wandered over to Iris for a sniff, but nothing about her had changed. It was strange. In all my experience with humans, I had never encountered one whose smells didn't fluctuate. I assumed it was the medication.

"How sweet. Your dog seems to care," Beatrice said.

"So Overton was not a nice person?" Harry asked.

"He was a horrible person."

The bluntness of Beatrice's comment seemed to awaken Iris.

"What would you know about him?" Iris asked. "Rumors swirled around but no one ever proved anything — nothing ever stuck — it was all cocktail party filth."

Iris squinted at something on the street below.

"How I do wish people would pick up after their dogs," she said and opened the window wider.

"Shame on you," she shouted.

The target of her complaint many stories below did not reply.

"Have you let Overton go?" Harry asked Beatrice.

"Let him go?"

Beatrice laughed. Her laugh was a hard

sound like the striking of rocks together.

"I never had to let him go. I never had a piece of him and he never had a piece of me."

Beatrice had spoken the last sentence softly, but Iris caught it. She gave Beatrice a sharp look, left the windowsill and disappeared into the bedroom.

"I have something that will shed true light on the man," Iris said over her shoulder.

"She's back among us mortals again," Beatrice said.

Iris returned with a small purse from which she extracted a piece of lavender-colored paper that had been folded into a little square. She held it up to Beatrice and Harry as if it were a precious stone.

"He gave this to me a few days before he died." Iris's voice cracked and hinted at tears, but the change of emotion in her voice was not matched by any change of smell in her person.

Iris opened the paper and began to read:

I am beginning to hate the sound of my own voice. I would be happiest silent, but then there are my thoughts. My thoughts carry the sound of my voice. Perhaps if I am silent long enough, long enough that I forget the sound of my own voice, then my thoughts will also forget its sound and someday assume a different sound. But such prolonged silence is not possible.

I am beginning to dislike my face. It is a hard face to look at. I've seen other similar faces and I dislike them also. My hands, they too offend me. The years seem to be stuck to them like honey or tar, both honey and tar. My hands have held babies, pickles, ice cream sandwiches, the daily newspaper and the dead. My hands are an indictment against me.

"This man struggled. This was a haunted man," Iris said. "He might have done others harm, but who hasn't? At heart he was a good man, a genuine man."

She folded the paper and returned it to her purse. A phrase from Imogen's journal came to my mind: *Overton says he fears for his life.* And I wondered what else besides his hands were an indictment against him.

"Dear, can I have another cigarette?" Iris addressed Beatrice, her tone suddenly airy again. "How I adore them."

Beatrice handed her a cigarette and Iris went back to the window.

"Smitten. Absolutely smitten," Beatrice said.

"It sounds like Overton was very aware of himself," Harry said. "Conscious of his flaws, that kind of thing."

"When it suited him. A writer — even a mediocre one — can make a corpse presentable," Beatrice said. "So is that it? Do you have everything you need? You know, I'm only doing this as a favor, because I like you. I don't believe a bit of this supernatural stuff and I have no idea what use any of this will be. Lyell died in that bathroom and now he's in a hole in Connecticut."

A Nephew is
Introduced
Things Get Even
Stranger

Then the doorbell rang. "That must be Michael coming for a New Year's visit," Iris said.

"Who's Michael?" Harry asked Beatrice.

"A nephew of sorts," Beatrice said, giving Harry a strange look.

The doorbell rang again. Beatrice rose and answered it.

A middle-aged man in a corduroy jacket entered the room. He carried a bouquet of red roses.

"Hello, Beatrice," he said. "Hello, Aunt Iris. Happy New Year — may it be profitable for us all!"

Then he noticed Harry and me and his mood grew instantly dark.

"Harry meet Michael," Beatrice said quickly. "Michael meet Harry. Harry's interests lie in the paranormal. He was here the night Overton died and has returned to follow up."

"What's to follow up?" Michael asked. "Overton died and was buried and he will *not* come again in glory."

"Harry thinks he might," Beatrice said. "Not in the body so much as in the spirit. He seems to think that he might return to haunt us."

"How do you go about becoming certified in the paranormal?" Michael asked.

"You don't," Harry said.

"So you don't have any real qualifications?"

"I've done a lot of reading and I've gone on calls."

"I see," Michael said. "So this is more hobby than anything else? You believe in this nonsense but not enough to try to earn a living at it."

"Well . . ."

"Never mind. I don't really care," Michael said.

There was an awkward silence.

Michael hung his jacket over the chair and handed Iris the flowers.

"Oh, dear. Michael always needs to confront. He's an Aries, of course, but that doesn't excuse it. I do apologize for his behavior, but *he* must as well," Iris said.

"What's the dog's name?" Michael asked.

The dog in question had sidled up to Michael. My tail wagged in apparent greeting, but my nose was in overdrive. Michael was shedding heavy doses of fear, anxiety and suspicion. Michael didn't like seeing Harry in the room, not at all. And he didn't like the apartment either because it reminded him of something that worried him very much. When he looked at Iris, however, I did notice a brief spike of attraction in an otherwise muted libido, but this was quickly overwhelmed by his more serious pre-occupations.

"His name is Randolph," Harry said.

Michael seized my chin and held my head up at a sharp angle.

"Randolph needs to trim down, doesn't he?" Michael said, moving my head up and down in the affirmative. "Randolph needs some exercise, doesn't he?"

I felt like biting his leg, but wrenched free instead.

"Randolph is a mellow dog," Harry warned. "But he has his limits."

"Michael, what's the matter?" Beatrice asked. "This isn't like you. I'm sorry, Harry, he's coming across like a brute but he's actually a professor of the decorative arts given to long-winded ruminations on brush-strokes and the application of glaze by eighteenth-century potters. Most of the time he's very civilized. Aren't you, Michael?"

Michael grunted.

"A drink will fix you up. I'm drinking sherry, what will you have?"

Beatrice was in the kitchen again, topping up her glass.

"Right . . . right . . . you're absolutely right," Michael said. "I'll have sherry, Beatrice. Thanks."

He turned to Harry.

"I am sorry, truly," Michael said. "Let's start again. Something about seeing people in the place where it happened and talking about Overton just bothers me . . ."

"Dear Michael despised Lyell, I'm afraid," Iris said.

"He was a phony," Michael snapped. "If he hadn't died of natural causes I might have killed him myself." As he said this, he reeked of that distinct masculine protectiveness men shed around women with whom they are intimate. But he didn't reek of the capacity for violence.

Beatrice handed Michael his sherry, and the professor of decorative arts sat down at the table.

"Well, Happy New Year," Michael toasted.

It was a strange bunch. An aging woman, growing slowly drunk on sherry, with an embarrassing interest in my owner and not a jot of self-consciousness; a woman of similar age seeming to fade in and out of sanity; a surly professor; and my young, handsome, melancholic and dangerously out-of-his-depth owner. It occurred to me that Harry could be sitting with three murderers.

Iris slid Harry's notebook across the table to him and smiled.

"You have such artistic handwriting," Iris said.

"You know the spirits have suggested that Overton was electrocuted," Harry mentioned.

Michael visibly flinched. Iris's and Beatrice's eyes met for a second.

"I think we've talked about Overton enough for one day," Beatrice said and turned to Michael. "Are you really going to Tortuga?"

"I most certainly am," Michael said.

"You're not taking your aunt along by chance?"

Iris smiled.

"You *are* taking your aunt!" Beatrice said. She clapped her hands together. "That's lovely, Michael. What a wonderful nephew."

"Wonderful in so many special ways," Iris said. Although nothing untoward passed between them above the table, under the table it was a different matter. Iris lifted one foot out of her shoe and fluttered it up Michael's pant leg. The distinct marking of remembered passion suffused the air. But Beatrice shed only the strong smell of confusion and worry. She finished her drink and poured another.

"So what do you do exactly?" Harry asked Michael.

"I study eighteenth-century plates and musical instruments. The two have absolutely nothing to do with one another and that's how I keep sane. Whenever I tire of stone, I turn to wood and vice versa. Violins are my subspecialty. Plates might go up in price, but violins soar."

"Why is that?" Harry asked.

"Supply and demand. You can see the same with other antiquities but violins stand out, because they are a practical artifact. No one is making an eighteenth-century Cremonese fiddle these days, are they? But the world is producing a mother lode of gifted musicians, and gifted musicians want to play the best. Mind you, the best isn't always Cremonese — they're just the most famous violins. There were dozens of great makers and then there were the Germans, who made an industry out of counterfeiting the Italian work. But even so, you're still left with a small pool of fine fiddles and a large and growing pool of fine musicians who want to play those fiddles."

Beatrice refilled her glass with sherry and lit her umpteenth cigarette.

"Iris, don't you have some of Lyell's china?" she asked.

"I'm certain it would have been nothing special," Michael scoffed.

"I didn't ask you, Michael," Beatrice said. "I asked Iris."

"Who gives a damn about the china?" Michael said.

"I'm sure that Irish would," Beatrice insisted. She was now quite drunk and beginning to slur her words. "Jush like I'm sure Irish would be intereshted in your recent flirtation with photography and its evidentiary consh . . . consh . . . consequences . . ."

Michael said nothing, but he emitted a distinct smell of fear.

"Dear, let's just enjoy our guests and this New Year for a while," Iris entreated.

She took my head in her palms. Her touch was very gentle and she ran her finger up and down under my neck, one of the most difficult places for Yours Truly to scratch.

"The universe is trying to tell us something through those eyes," Iris said dreamily. "And I don't have the foggiest idea what it is."

Randolph Considers the Question of Drunkenness A Woman is Threatened

Harry and I had left Beatrice, Michael and Iris in a state of great conflict thanks to Harry's bomb-dropping comment about electrocution. Soon after Iris made her enigmatic observation about my eyes and the universe, she had vanished into the bedroom without a word to anyone and not re-emerged. Beatrice was beyond conversation at this point and Michael had veered back toward being inhospitable. He had stalked to the far corner of the room and sunk into a chair. Harry decided to take our leave for which my bladder was very thankful.

With the exception of a stray drop or two of Harry's Heineken in my water bowl, I have never experimented with alcohol in any real way. But it is clear from my observation of human behavior that alcohol is a powerful confounder of the human being. It is easy to dismiss a drunk's sluggish body and sloppy words, but I hold with the ancients: *In vino veritas.* In wine is truth and there was much truth to consider following Beatrice's sherry-fueled words. She was clearly threatened by Michael and Iris's relationship and by their prospective trip to Tortuga. What did the reference to Overton's china mean? Or Michael's photography? Or evidentiary consequences?

Harry had gone to bed early, but I followed these traces into the forest of possibility until the garbage trucks made their thunderous metallic rounds down our street. It was already dawn.

Shadows engulfed the table, the refrigerator, the easels and the canvases, the vertically stacked books and tilting piles of magazines, making them look like objects in some strange procession of the dead. But I realized that I had emerged from this tangle of possibility knowing something concrete. Another message was required.

Harry might rise at any moment. Holmes needed to work quickly. I nudged the chair into place with a minimum of screeching. Soon the message read:

BEATRICE AND MICHAEL HAD STAKE IN
OVERTON DEATH

Then something unexpected happened. The downstairs buzzer rang. I thought it must be a mistake. Sometimes people push the wrong button; other times they push all the buttons hoping that someone will forget their big city instincts and let a stranger inside — the Holly Golightly syndrome. But this individual was incredibly persistent. In addition to my fatigue, I felt a headache coming on — a Labrador's starts at the very tips of his ears. Finally Harry stumbled from the bedroom and pushed the intercom.

"Who is it?" he croaked.

"Beatrice," a strained and desperate female voice announced.

"She's found me," Harry groaned.

"Please let me in."

Harry buzzed Beatrice through the downstairs door. Soon I heard her footsteps on the stairs. They didn't sound like the footsteps I had associated with this woman. These were heavy, plodding, old footsteps. These were grudging feet carrying a difficult cargo up the stairs. I hoped Harry would see the messages on the kitchen table and hide them. Instead, he ran to his bedroom to throw on some clothes.

Beatrice arrived at our front door. Harry had left it ajar and she pushed it open.

"Knock, knock."

"Come in," Harry called from the bedroom.

Beatrice seemed to have suffered a general collapse. Gone was the sense of youthfulness framed by gray. The skin around her eyes, neck and cheeks had been taut and flush, now it was pale and cascading over itself. She reeked of worry, fear and residual sherry. Something had turned the Kwo Bo expert into a broken and terrified woman overnight.

Harry emerged from the bedroom.

"Aren't you the brightest thing to walk into my day?" Beatrice said weakly.

"What's going on?" Harry asked.

"I'm brash. I know I am, but I would never have come here unless I had a very good reason. I found your address at Iris's. I guess you wrote it down on one of your visits."

"That's right," Harry said.

Beatrice began to shake and tears formed in her eyes. She took a deep breath.

"Michael attacked me," she said.

"What?" Harry asked.

"He wants to kill me. I know it. I'm going nuts with fear. I stepped over every crack on the way here. Every crack on the sidewalk. And I counted them all. Do you know how many cracks there are?"

Harry shrugged.

"Two hundred and eighty-six."

"Interesting."

"It's not interesting. It's crazy. My dad was a psychiatrist — he would say I was having a breakdown."

Harry guided Beatrice into Grandfather Oswald's Laz-Z-Boy.

"I didn't even know that they made these things anymore," Beatrice said as she settled back into the extraordinarily comfortable invention.

"Try the leg rest," Harry offered, lifting it into place.

He disappeared into the bedroom and emerged with a sports blanket from his undergraduate days. He handed Beatrice the blanket and she tucked it around herself.

"Do you want some tea?" Harry asked.

Our guest nodded and then she noticed me.

"Hi, doggy. Don't you just turn up everywhere."

Beatrice held my head. She pinched my ears and twisted my fur around her fingers. It was very unpleasant, but I permitted it out of sympathy.

Harry found the kettle beneath a week's accumulation of mail and filled it with water from the tap.

"I can trust you, can't I?" Beatrice asked.

"Sure."

Beatrice pulled the blanket up to her chin.

"Michael's not really Iris's nephew."

"He's not?" Harry was quite surprised. His dog was not.

"No. Do you have a cigarette?"

"Sorry."

Harry had once again exhausted his emergency cigarette stash.

"A smoke-free artist — I'm shocked. That is what you really are, isn't it? Not some hokey ghost hunter. You're a painter. I found you on Google. Quite the up-and-ccoming last year: a show at Gallery 1515 and Arcadia in the same month — a real coup."

"That was just hype. Google, huh?"

Harry looked mournfully over at the closet where he had stowed the laptop after Imogen's disappearance. He hadn't been on the Internet for a very long time.

"The fellowships weren't hype, were they?"

"The only thing that matters is what you produce."

"You're a beautiful boy, but I'm sure you produced something — they didn't have you stand in the middle of an empty gallery and look pretty."

Harry lowered himself onto a hassock at Beatrice's feet.

"I don't want to talk about me," Harry said. "What did Michael do to you?"

"I'll get to that in a second. I just need a minute. Let's talk about something else."

"Okay," Harry said. "So Michael and Iris aren't related?"

"Iris always was a bit of a whore."

"They're lovers?"

"Most certainly."

"Why do they pretend not to be?"

"Iris is big on propriety. Wear the black armband, play the mourning widow for the appropriate period. Besides they had gotten used to the roles. They were playing them all along. When Michael and Iris met last year, hiding was necessary."

"Iris was with Overton and Michael at the same time?"

"Yes."

"I thought Iris would have been loyal to Overton."

"She was loyal in her own fashion."

"What did Michael think?"

"There was nobody happier than Michael when Lyell dropped dead. Nobody on the planet. God, he said as much yesterday. He wanted Iris all to himself. Michael is even jealous of me. I guess I remind him of Lyell. He wants Iris to be done with him once and for all."

"Will she be done with him?"

"Never."

The teakettle began to whistle and Harry excused himself. He clanked about the drawers but couldn't find a tea bag and returned to the hassock.

"Sorry, I thought I had some tea, but I don't," Harry said.

"That's fine."

She rolled up both sleeves, revealing yellowish bruises on each forearm about the size of a man's fingerprints.

"Michael did that to you?" Harry asked.

"And this." Beatrice pulled down the neck of her turtleneck sweater to display an eggplant-stain on her shoulder. "I can hardly rotate my arm it's so painful. He punched me in the stomach too, but that doesn't leave a mark."

What had happened to the Kwo Bo champion in the face of such aggression? I thought. Harry wondered the same thing.

"Aren't you a martial arts expert?"

"Kwo Bo's more of a body wholeness sort of thing. It's an art form, really, where mind and body seek union through intentional motion. I can fight another Kwo Bo practitioner because they would know what they were doing, but it doesn't work against sloppy violence."

I was reminded of Mark Twain's marvelous observation: *The best swordsman in the world has nothing to fear from the second best swordsman in the world, but he may very well be killed by the fool who has picked up a sword for the first time and is just messing about with it.*

"Michael pushed me up against the bookcase and then he threatened me."

"Did you scream?" Harry asked.

"It happened too fast. When I doubled over, he came up and sort of put his hand on the back of my head and yanked it up and then looked into my eyes. He looked utterly deranged. I have never liked Michael, but this wasn't even Michael, it was someone else entirely. He didn't say he wanted me to stay away from Iris. He didn't say that he never wanted me to mention Lyell again. He didn't even say that he hated me or he wished that I was dead. All he said was 'I'll do it later.' I'm never going to forget those words as long as I live. 'I'll do it later.' They were so matter-of-fact, like killing me was something that he had decided on a long time before, a fait accompli."

"Then what happened?"

"Iris was in the bedroom and he went

there. I got up off the floor and pulled myself into a chair. It felt like I was sitting there forever. It was awful. I thought my stomach was going to burst. God, it hurt so much. Then Michael came out of the bedroom, got his coat and walked out the door. He didn't even look at me. I thought I might get my things together and go home but before I did, I went in to check on Iris. She was sound asleep. Michael had left a note on the bedside table for her to find when she awoke. Sappy nonsense, the kind of thing that lovers write to one another and are never embarrassed by. No mention of roughing up her friend of course or threatening her life."

"And then you went home?"

"No. I stayed on the couch overnight. I was just too scared to leave. It was about nine when Michael attacked me. I mean it was early and I kept thinking Iris would wake up, but she slept through the entire night. I didn't fall asleep for a second."

Although Daisy Mae, that monstrous Great Dane, is not a dog of whom I am fond, I thought of her vast unemptied bladder and the agony of waiting into the early hours for Beatrice's return. An accident under the circumstances would have been quite understandable.

"Why didn't you call the police?" Harry asked.

"What would they do? Get a restraining order? I had that experience long ago. You're never really protected. If someone wants to kill you, they'll kill you."

Beatrice began to sob. There was a nuance of smells about her that made me think her tears didn't stem from the present situation with Michael.

"I don't know what to tell you," my owner said.

"There's nothing *to* tell me, doll. I feel old. I feel spent. I feel scared."

I could smell my owner's mind. He didn't like Beatrice very much. He trusted her even less, but her fear seemed authentic to him and in the parlance of conmen and other exploiters of human nature, Harry was a soft touch. In other words, he was buying the story hook, line and *bloody* sinker. For my part, I could imagine the menacing figure from Christmas night coming up the stairs at any moment. Perhaps he was already outside our door.

"What do you need?" Harry asked softly.

"Someone to watch over me," Beatrice said, but then quickly added, "but I don't want to ruin your life."

"There's not much left to ruin."

"Can you come to my lecture tonight?" Beatrice asked. "It's actually a lecture slash book signing slash meet and greet. Connie Tapas, the famous literary agent, is supposed to show."

"Where?"

"The Barnes & Noble at Lincoln Square. Could you do that for me, babe?"

"Sure," Harry said. "But it doesn't seem like much."

"Oh, it means a lot more than you know," Beatrice said.

During the long silence that followed, I noted how a certain relief had begun to settle in for Beatrice. I hoped that it was not the kind of relief that someone has after someone else has walked straight into their trap.

"I feel a lot better now," Beatrice finally said.

Then to my horror, her eyes fell on the kitchen table. I had contemplated gobbling up the messages as Beatrice climbed the stairs, but there had been no time.

"Playing with cereal?" Beatrice asked.

"What?" Harry asked. But Yours Truly had already sprung (or rather proceeded) into action.

"What a strange dog," Beatrice exclaimed.

The strange dog in question had decided

that the message must be destroyed and at some injury to himself had delivered a heavy blow to a leg of the table with all seventy-seven pounds of his well-fed, profoundly unexercised body. Cereal spilled off the surface onto the floor scattering everywhere, but, as I learned a split second later, the job was incomplete and the bulk of the messages remained.

"Are you writing about me in cereal?" Beatrice asked.

She tried to peer around Harry who stood between her and the table.

"It's nothing. Just random thoughts that I jot down."

Beatrice read a significant snippet aloud.

" 'Possible foul play four people involved one is Beatrice.' What is that supposed to mean? Foul play involving who?"

At this critical juncture, my owner impressed me with the creativity of his evasion.

"It's just spirit talk, a metaphor for an unsettled or accidental death. I was trying to channel Overton's mystic force and that is what came out."

"But why cereal?"

"It's also mixed media art. Furniture and food. The spiritual influence represents a twist on the classic representation of the muse in art. The cereal represents the momentary and passing quality of elements of the physical world and the furniture represents the basis or support, the sturdier physicality of the world — the bedrock upon which passing art can be fashioned."

Beatrice tried to push past Harry.

"Please let me read," she insisted.

"It's unfinished."

"The precious artiste," Beatrice said. "My father was an artist, I understand."

"I thought you said your father was a psychiatrist."

"That was his day job, but his passion was sculpture. Vocation as opposed to avocation."

I smelled strong waves of evasion and deceit as Beatrice donned her coat and moved toward the door.

"I'll see you tonight," she said.

"What time?"

"Seven-thirty in the second-floor reading room."

"I'll be there," Harry said.

"That electrocution idea was cute," Beatrice said. "If only Michael was that clever."

Then she was gone, leaving the apartment to settle into some degree of serenity as her scent trail slowly vanished. Harry searched again and managed to find both a tea bag and a cigarette. He reignited the kettle and he bent his face down to the stove top and lit the cigarette on the burner. Then he pushed the chair up to the kitchen table and sat down before the latest skewed but still readable message.

I spent ten minutes fruitlessly putting Imogen's code through the paces of a ROT 13 Caesar cipher until Harry snapped his fingernail against his mug making a lovely bell-like sound. The mug was one of those novelty gifts for which Imogen had a penchant. She had purchased it on the boardwalk in Ocean Bluff, New Jersey, one early June weekend before the crowds turned the place into an unbearable honky-tonk parade of funnel cakes, saltwater taffy and soft serve ice cream. It read: *Proud Father of a Labrador Retriever* beneath a picture of a rather pudgy member of my kind. She was a funny girl, our Imogen, given to intricate explorations of the most intellectual topics yet completely helpless when it came to buying the silliest kitsch. There were stacks of Franklin Mint Commemorative Ice Capades plates, a dozen Superman lint removers, and every free electrical outlet in our apartment featured a plastic air freshener/night light in the shape of one of the twelve apostles. There was even a Judas.

Harry Goes Blind
Gravity Shows its
Ugly Side

New York at the beginning of the New Year presents a grim face. Holiday decorations disappear from public places and store windows, the gray winter settles in and the sidewalks are crowded with an isolated people, each inhabiting his or her own separate, purpose-filled universe. Without any of the collective cheer or last-minute hysteria of the holidays, people suddenly find themselves deep in winter, enduring the routines that must see them through to spring. A general weariness descends. It is especially palpable in the early evening when a certain bad humor seems closer to the surface. Unfortunately for Harry and me this was precisely the time we attempted to sneak into Barnes & Noble.

"Can I help you, sir?" the security guard asked with a sharp confrontational tone in his voice and a scent of alpha male aggression so strong my fur immediately stood on end. Harry kept walking, but the guard blocked his way.

How long had I desired to enter this bookstore? How many times had Harry hurried me past during one of our extended walks around the city? From dozens of spots on the surrounding sidewalks, one can glimpse the expanse of shelf after book-crammed shelf, the promise of cozy nooks and hidden corners, the great continuum of philosophy, history, literature, cooking and gardening books climbing level by level to the pinnacle: a magazine-lined coffee shop where whole afternoons and evenings could be whiled away over a single beverage if only one were a biped.

Harry ignored the guard's first challenge and walked straight into the man.

"You can't bring a dog in here, sir."

"But this is my dog."

"I can see that."

"My special guard dog."

"You can't bring a guard dog into the store even if it's special."

"Did I say guard dog? I meant guide dog. You see I'm blind."

Harry waved a hand in front of his face as if the gesture would highlight this fact.

"See?"

The guard did not. My owner might have

looked ridiculous in Imogen's Jackie O sunglasses, but I tried to appear a bit more disciplined by sucking in my stomach and pointing in the appropriate direction.

"That ain't the right leash either. The ones for guide dogs are more like a harness."

"It's a new thing. More humane to the animal."

"You tryin' to be a comedian?"

"I don't think you should harass me for my disability. If you want, I'll take an eye test. Then I'll file my lawsuit."

The word *lawsuit* gave the guard pause. His resistance vanished.

"You're cool," the guard said. "Ain't nobody harassing you. I'm just doin' my job. Where you need to go?"

"Kwo Bo lecture."

"Top of the escalator and straight ahead."

Harry and I rose on the escalator into the sublime upper levels of the bookstore. The smell of so many books was a heady one and I forgot myself at the top of the escalator, causing Harry to hop over me when I stopped dead in my tracks.

"Randolph," Harry hissed, "pay attention."

We navigated through the shelves. To maintain the illusion of a blind man and his dog, Harry managed to clip three displays and topple a cardboard Eiffel Tower advertising the new best-selling diet book *Cigarette d'Jour: Why the French Don't Get Fat.*

After a few more circular and catastrophic perambulations, we arrived at our destination. Every seat in the reading room was occupied by women who looked like they each had at least one marriage behind them but maintained a desperate desire, dying a little every day, that something in the way of love may yet be salvaged. In the meantime, they would fortify their personal castles and arm themselves to the teeth for the inevitable onslaught of sharks and/or leeches into which two categories members of the opposite sex fell. Kwo Bo fit neatly into this worldview with its emphasis on self-esteem, sinewy bodies and the promise of flamboyant violence against a host of threats. A few slump-shouldered men were inexplicably scattered through this burgeoning crowd. No one of either gender offered up their chair for the young blind man so Harry squeezed his large frame between the display poster and the doorframe.

Seven-thirty came and went with no sign of Beatrice. At seven thirty-five the crowd began to get restless. When a crowd gets restless — especially this particular type of Manhattan crowd — patience is drowned in hyperactivity. Conversations and arguments erupt between strangers and long cell phone monologues ensue during which the politics and sex lives of many present are revealed in microscopic detail. By seven-forty a few people had stormed out muttering like the deranged. Finally, one woman went to find the manager.

"This is ridiculous. I've got a life, you know," she informed everyone present as she disappeared.

I had begun to worry about the Kwo Bo expert's well-being when I was shocked to see Michael arrive and make his way to the back of the room where he leaned against the wall.

But I had no time to contemplate Michael's presence because in a tumbling blur of heavy white cotton, Beatrice appeared. Howling, punching and kicking, she raced toward the podium. The woman who came to rest behind the lectern looked nothing like the frightened creature who had arrived on our doorstep that morning. Her hair had been colored, lengthened and braided down her back. Her face looked twenty years younger and beamed with teenage freshness. From what I could see of her arms beneath the loose sleeves of her martial arts outfit, her bruises had even disappeared.

Beatrice wore a mobile microphone that enabled her to race about the room. She offered no apology for her lateness.

"How are those energy levels out there tonight?"

Some head-shaking, a nod, a smattering of fatigued smiles greeted the question.

"Tired? Stupid question, Beatrice. Of course I'm tired. It's the middle of winter. The holidays are over. Miserable, wet, cold days out there and the same crap at work and at home or wherever. Of course my energy levels are in the gutter. They're zero. They're *below* zero."

Beatrice paced, skipped and broke into a jog. She was part of the crowd but somehow high above it at the same time.

"I hear you and I'm here to help. I'm here to tell you exactly how Kwo Bo can beat those winter blues and just about every other kind of blues you have. I guarantee you that if you were doing Kwo Bo right now, so much of that stuff — that crap — would just melt away. Your energy levels would go stratospheric. Absolutely stratospheric."

Three minutes into Beatrice's presentation I felt a profound inertia settle over me. I find such hyperactive showmanship exhausting. I am not inclined to much energy in any case, but this kind of spectacle seems a disappointing, almost evolutionary, step backward. Why must the promoter pretend that nothing else exists in the world besides this product — *his* Five-in-One Potato Peeler or *her* Custom Chrome Polish? It is as if what passes for progress is just wiping the collective memory clean again and again to make room for the next moronic device, technique or "breakthrough."

Yet, surveying the room as Beatrice droned on in her predictable ecstasy, it was obvious to see that many of the people had really been won over. Even Manhattan, I am ashamed to say, with its baseline of urban sophistication has its fair share of the gullible and the absurd. They had been looking for the next big thing and they thought they had found it in Beatrice. The legacy of fatigue and low energy levels was finally to be cured by a few roundhouse kicks and some breathing exercises. Bravo. Nor should one forget to employ the accompanying mantra: *"A Strong Woman Is a Happy Woman."* I did not recall ever before hearing these words on Beatrice's own lips, but soon the whole room buzzed as the audience repeated them on the Kwo Bo expert's cue. By this point I had curled up into a ball at my owner's feet with a fatigue that surpasses understanding. A demonstration followed in which Beatrice broke a board with her middle finger and put the bookstore manager in a headlock.

It was difficult to see Michael from my spot by the door. Beatrice often had the crowd on its feet. But in the moments that I could see him, I was struck by how unthreatening he appeared. This man did not look like a would-be murderer. Of course he could be a psychopath, one of those craven smoothies who have terrified humanity since the beginning of time. I had never smelled a psychopath, but I suspected that one must smell quite different from a normal person. Michael's scents had suggested extremes of emotion and perhaps a guilty or anxious conscience. And Beatrice's story, if true, revealed a man who was dangerous, susceptible to certain passions. Was he a psychopath, though? I doubted it, but we would soon find out. I hoped painlessly.

The talk ended with a book signing. All the high energy spilled out the doors of the reading room and into the New York night that absorbed it like a sponge. Michael vanished with the crowd. I was fairly certain he had seen us, but I had the distinct sense that my owner had somehow missed him.

Beatrice stood amid a gaggle of admirers and regaled them with Kwo Bo anecdotes until she excused herself to speak with a short woman in the corner. Harry and I remained along the wall.

Beatrice called from across the room.

"Meet Connie Tapas, the world's greatest agent."

Harry, keeping up the blindman act, extended his arm in the wrong direction as we weaved across the room to reach the pair.

"Hello."

"What on earth are you doing?" Beatrice asked.

"He's playing blind so he can have a dog up here. Amusing," the whip smart super literary agent Connie Tapas surmised. Her casual tone suggested she saw this kind of thing every day.

"That dog goes everywhere with you, doesn't he?" Beatrice said. "If only *I* could have the same permission. I promise I'd behave."

She turned to Connie. "He's a dream isn't he?"

"A dream," Connie echoed.

"What did you think, Harry? Did I knock them dead?"

Harry nodded.

"See their faces when I mentioned how

my fifteen minute abdominal exercise can burn three hundred calories and lower your blood pressure? Made it up on the spot. Catch that, Connie?"

"Caught it."

Connie turned to go. "Nice crowd. Nice buzz," she said. "I'll call you."

The agent walked out of the room.

"So that means you're interested?" Beatrice called after her.

Connie Tapas disappeared down the escalator without another word.

"Is that your agent?" Harry asked.

"Sort of. She's wildly interested but her plate is full."

A janitor began to arrange the chairs. He shook his head at the fragments of the broken board on the podium.

"This yours?" he asked Beatrice.

"Oh no, gumdrop, just a prop."

The janitor threw the fragments into his rolling trashcan with a grunt of disapproval.

"Let's go," Beatrice said. "We're obviously not wanted here."

The wave of public-speaking euphoria had broken and stranded Beatrice back in reality. Beatrice began to slip into the more vulnerable and broken state that we had seen that morning.

As we exited the building, Beatrice

clutched Harry's arm.

"Did you see him?" she demanded.

"Who?"

"Michael, for God's sake. He was at my talk, standing against the back wall, grinning like a lunatic."

"Really?"

"You *are* blind," Beatrice said. "Do you think you can walk me home? I'm shaky again. I know it's a lot to ask."

We walked a few more blocks in silence. I searched out the shadows for Michael but he was nowhere to be seen or smelled.

"You were good," Harry said.

Beatrice shrugged. "You think? They didn't buy many books."

"I didn't know that you could break a board with your middle finger."

Beatrice shrugged again. "Doll, the only thing that matters is people putting their dollars up for a book. Asses in the seats don't pay the rent or put food on the table. This goddamn city is filled with people whose social lives revolve around getting as much free entertainment as possible."

"I think you're being too hard on yourself," Harry said.

"Thanks. That's sweet," Beatrice said. "I can't believe you didn't see Michael."

She lit a cigarette and her first exhale filled

the air with a great cloud of smoke. The digital billboard above the bank at Seventy-second Street read fifteen degrees. Water had frozen along the curbs and in a few dirty slicks on the sidewalks. The Alberta Clipper, a notorious front of arctic air that settles over Manhattan two or three times a year, had arrived. Temperatures would drop into the single digits and possibly far below.

"I'm sick of winter," Beatrice said. "If I had my way, I'd live somewhere warm. Boca, maybe, or the Caribbean. Anywhere but New York in January. This town is miserable if you don't have money. It wasn't always like that. I used to have money. Lots and lots of money. Fifty years later the debutante of 1954 depends on rent control, social security and smokes the cheapest cigarettes she can find. Would you believe I lived in the Ansonia when I was a kid?"

Beatrice gestured at the Beaux Arts masterpiece as we hurried across Seventy-second Street on the blinking red man. The building, always a favorite of mine, is one of the greatest examples of fin-de-siècle Manhattan architecture. In its curves, flourishes and sloping roofline I can detect all the hope and belief in the inevitability of human progress that preceded the dismal carnage of the twentieth century.

"Way out of my price range," Beatrice mourned.

We walked at a clip up Amsterdam Avenue. The bars and restaurants were quiet on this cold weeknight.

"All those people at the bookstore looking for answers. It's kind of sad really. I'd die if they knew I smoked. Then that bitch Connie Tapas gave me the bird. Well, good for her. There are other fish in the sea. I'll make some calls tomorrow and we'll see about the next book. Connie will be dying to represent me."

Beatrice froze and grabbed Harry's shoulder. The scent of fear that had been momentarily diluted by frustration now returned swamping the milder emotion with its power.

"Michael," she hissed.

"Where?" Harry asked.

"There. On the opposite side of the street. He just ducked into that bodega. I swear it was him."

I had seen no one.

"We shouldn't just stand here," Harry said.

"Can I stay at your place?" Beatrice asked.

It was obvious that Harry was not fond of the idea.

"Are you sure we shouldn't go to the

police?" Harry asked.

"I'll sleep on the couch. I promise I won't be a bother. I'll even clean up."

"I get up early for work," Harry said, taking liberties with the truth of his flexible freelance schedule.

"I'll be out before that."

"Let's just keep moving and we'll see how things go," Harry decided.

We hurried up the avenue, but had only covered a few more blocks when Beatrice stopped to light another cigarette. Her hand was shaking and she kept looking behind her as if Michael would appear at any moment. To distract herself, I suppose, she began to hold forth on what might have been her basic philosophy of human nature.

"People are neither good nor bad. It's all about how they see themselves."

Beatrice inhaled the cigarette smoke deeply.

"I'm somewhere in between. I want to see myself as good but if I'm honest I have to say that —"

Beatrice didn't have a chance to apply her philosophical premise to herself because at that moment a 10,000 BTU air conditioner, freed from its window housing fifteen stories above her head, was plunging toward the sidewalk. Given the weight of the appliance and the rules of physics, had Beatrice remained standing in the same spot she would have soon been compressed vertically into the sidewalk and been no more. Instead, a sharp warning cry issued out of the darkness. Harry glanced skyward, assessed the situation and with superb athleticism heaved the smoking Kwo Bo expert well out of the way while simultaneously throwing himself and his leashed dog to safety. The air conditioner smashed into the sidewalk turning into a shattered mess of broken coils, vents and fans.

In any other metropolis, this would be a moment for stunned silence, but New York doesn't lend itself to quiet reflection after disasters. Taxis honked and clattered and pedestrians who had not seen the event stepped around the scene unaware of what had just happened. Harry picked himself off the sidewalk and left me to drag my leash along the ground as he checked on Beatrice. She was propped against the building. Her broken cigarette dangled from her lips. She stared at the heap of metal and plastic on the sidewalk a few feet away.

"My God," she muttered.

"Are you in pain?" Harry asked. Beatrice's legs were splayed out on the sidewalk like the limbs of a broken mannequin.

She contemplated them.

"You mean these old things?" she asked.

Beatrice straightened them out with a grunt.

"Trick hips," she explained.

By this time a small crowd of people had gathered, including the doorman and the building's superintendent. A patrol car arrived. Speculation and finger-pointing began. Beatrice lit a fresh cigarette and leaned into the building while Harry consulted with the police officers.

"Happens all the time," one of the policemen said. "We get three of these calls a week. It's an epidemic. Problem is people don't screw these bad boys in and then vibrations cause them to slip."

"But it's the middle of winter," Beatrice said. "Why on earth would anyone have their air conditioner running?"

"They overheat apartments in Manhattan," the doorman said. "People use their air conditioners straight through winter. Ain't that so, Manny?"

The superintendent seconded this assertion and added the following legalistic reflection that he seemed to have memorized:

"We do what we can to make sure the tenants secure their units, but in the final analysis the units are their responsibility. We can't be held accountable for every nut that's loose and every screw that falls out nor for the negligence of individual owners who fail to follow standard safety procedures."

"I have never heard such nonsense," Beatrice said.

She turned to Harry and spoke in an urgent whisper. "I told you Michael had the power to kill me."

Beatrice scanned the crowd as if one of the onlookers might pull off a latex mask at any moment and reveal Michael beneath.

"Beatrice, how could Michael arrange this? It's too random."

"It just looks random. That's the genius of it."

One of the officers overheard Beatrice's suggestion.

"Lady, you sayin' that this wasn't an accident?"

"That's exactly what I'm *sayin'*."

"Are you makin' fun of the way I speak?"

"Of course not."

"Not everyone is born and bred on the Upper West Side, Miss Silver Spoon."

"Unfortunately," Beatrice hissed.

"What?"

The strain of the past twenty-four hours

finally got the better of the Kwo Bo expert and she let fly.

"My God, there doesn't seem to be a single brain cell at work here. If there was, a certain man would now be in custody and I would be safe. Isn't it obvious that someone is trying to kill me? Can no one understand this?"

As a dog I am at a sufficient remove to detect those moments when the human species begins to behave like a pack instead of individual creatures. Aldous Huxley referred to these group tendencies as "herd poisoning." As Beatrice railed on against the assembled crowd, I witnessed the people quickly become of one poisonous mind. It completely forgot about the shattered air conditioner or Beatrice's close encounter with death. It focused instead on her shrill delivery and odd appearance, forming certain negative conclusions about her credibility and her sanity. Unfortunately, these conclusions were promptly supported by two events.

The first involved the arrival of a large man in a powder blue bathrobe. This man, it seemed, had been responsible for the plunging air conditioner. The unit, he readily admitted, had not been properly secured to its housing (though he noted that he was not mechanically inclined and could not tell the difference between a flat head screwdriver and a Phillips head). He assumed complete responsibility for the catastrophe and actually began to cry when he related knocking against said unit with his rear as he flamenco danced in his living room. As a result of the bump, the air conditioner had promptly slid off its housing and fallen the fifteen stories to the street. The scream that had warned us of the impending disaster had also come from the man in the powder blue bathrobe.

"I am truly sorry," the man said. "What can I do to make it better?"

He was telling the truth. Overpowering the smell of French cologne and moisturizer were the scents of contrition, honesty and trauma. Beatrice, however, would not be assuaged. This led to the second event that hardened opinion against her.

"Arrest him."

"Lady, please," the policeman begged.

"Is that your air conditioner or is it not?" Beatrice asked.

"I'm afraid it is. I'm very sorry," the man in the powder blue bathrobe murmured.

"There's the evidence," Beatrice said. "What more do you need?"

She pushed her finger into the policeman's chest.

"I'm telling you they're out to kill me. I give you proof and all you do is stand there. You're a disgrace."

"Beatrice, settle down," Harry urged.

But Beatrice did not settle down. Instead she put the policeman in a Kwo Bo–inspired headlock. The officer showed remarkable restraint as he disentangled himself from the woman and immobilized her against the wall. Thankfully, our narrow island of Manhattan is graced by a marvelous police force. But even the officer's admirable forbearance did not prevent him from deciding that something more must be done. Beatrice's aggression coupled with the fact that she was wearing a karate outfit beneath her overcoat compelled him to call for medical support.

Three minutes later an ambulance arrived and disgorged two EMTs with a carry chair. Beatrice was "assisted" into the chair, secured by means of belts and her vital signs taken.

"But there's nothing wrong with me," Beatrice screamed.

"Another one for the cuckoo closet, gentlemen," the police officer directed.

"Harry, tell them I'm not crazy."

"Officer, does this really need to happen?"

"She attacked me."

"But she's not usually like that."

"How do you know her?"

"I met her at a séance."

"Right." The police officer scrutinized Harry as if perhaps he might need to call a second ambulance. "Look, my friend, there's worse things than going to the flight deck for a cooldown."

"Flight deck?"

"Mental ward. There's worse things than the flight deck. Three hots and a cot and antianxiety medication. She could be going to the Tombs for assaulting an officer. Your lady friend should consider herself lucky."

"She's not my lady friend," Harry said.

Beatrice was deposited in the back of the ambulance.

"Harry, don't leave me," Beatrice screamed.

"Can I at least ride with her?" Harry asked the policeman.

"It's up to you. But it won't help none. You won't be able to see her at the hospital. I guarantee you she'll be going into lockup overnight."

Beatrice had begun to howl and fought with the straps that kept her bound to the chair.

"Definitely an overnighter," the officer said. "If I was you, I'd go home, get some sleep and drop in at the hospital sometime mid afternoon."

The crowd had dispersed. Even the man in the powder blue bathrobe had gotten too cold and vanished. The superintendent had already loaded the remains of the air conditioner on a dolly and was sweeping up the last of the scattered metal.

"Harry, please don't leave me!" Beatrice screamed.

Harry was about to disregard the policeman's advice and step into the ambulance, but the EMT stopped him.

"No dogs," he said, pointing at me.

Harry gave Beatrice a helpless look as the doors of the ambulance closed. The vehicle blasted its siren and was gone. The policeman had Harry make a statement. Then my owner and I turned toward home.

Harry planned to drop me there and then see what he could do for Beatrice at the hospital. He hoped to get her released that night. I was less optimistic. The woman had shown a brittle side and the system had its way of doing things with the hysterical and the aggressive. Once in its clutches, a swift exit was unlikely from the vast nocturnal network of the city's mental health machine.

We traveled north on Amsterdam Avenue. Home was still many blocks away, and I worried what dangers we might yet encounter before we arrived. But I also imagined our great city stretching out all around and above us. What diversities and similarities: the evil and the good drinking glasses of warm milk and tucking themselves into bed; junkies preparing needles in high rises and tenements alike; children wondering for the first time whether the universe they could barely see through the urban light was infinite. And among all of these, one person or more might be guilty of the murder of a famous writer who was not very kind. A woman was being hospitalized for insanity but not for the rashness, egotism and blarney from which she actually suffered. And a man and his dog were as lost as everybody else.

As per usual, verse sprang to mind, this time from the contemporary master, Francis Jani, and his short poem of Manhattan and that East River highway named after our thirty-second President, "No Weeping on the FDR." I always imagine the speaker of the poem high above the metropolis looking out on the vast spill of lights, struck by the imponderable complexity of the human condition he believes exists within the vista but remains nevertheless invisible to him: *Each lit window is a wicked jewel of the race. / In Bellevue souls chew off their tongues;/ at the Plaza a virgin's buttons are undone. /The waters of the Eastern river flex/ like the tarry sinews of a god.*

Bellevue was the infamous mental ward at the great city hospital to which Beatrice was currently in transit. I hoped that she might be shielded from its grimmer visions.

When we arrived home, Harry extracted the New Year's leftovers from the still deeply troubled refrigerator and put them in my bowl for my dinner. He was about to head downtown to the hospital when the telephone rang and we were both greatly surprised.

BEATRICE FINDS A SAFE HOUSE
A DOG DOES YOGA
AGAINST HIS WILL

The caller was Beatrice and she had gotten home before we had. It was not her home, but allow me to explain.

Traffic to the hospital had come to a standstill after a water-main break turned three blocks on Ninth Avenue into a sheet of ice. Beatrice had managed to calm herself down sufficiently to enable her to explain to the EMTs what had happened with the air conditioner and why she was wearing a karate outfit. By chance one of them recognized her from a Learning Center brochure.

"You're the Kwo Bo lady. Wicked cool."

This fact convinced the EMTs that their charge should be released. They cancelled the call and put Beatrice in a taxi to our home. But she didn't go to our home. Instead, she went to her own. Something about the trauma had made her momentarily fearless. Beatrice planned to spend the night in her own bed. She said she didn't care if Michael was waiting to finish off the job. But as the adrenaline began to ebb from her system, she became convinced that this was foolhardy. She was about to walk out the door and come to us when an old friend called. This man was a wealthy collector of oversized editions of classic books that he housed in the extraordinary library of his Fifth Avenue apartment. No offense, she told Harry, but the collector was her first choice for guest accommodations given her long intimacy with him.

"No offense taken," Harry said.

She was feeling fabulous, Beatrice concluded. Just fabulous. She said she would check in with him in a day or so.

Harry hung up the phone, got a beer from the refrigerator and caught the end of the news in the La-Z-Boy. Our solitude had been preserved and without Beatrice's incarceration in Bellevue as a mental case.

The television droned on and I fell into a light snooze, but then my ears pricked up at a segment on yoga classes for Manhattan dogs. The Pooch Palace — Canine Pool and Spa, my swimming club, was featured. The perky reporter discoursed thus: *Chakras aren't just for humans anymore. Doggies can keep up with their owners as the yoga craze continues to spread. Now Fido can stretch both paw and spirit. This is Zest Kilpatrick for* Channel 8 — News on the Eight.

"Hey, there's an idea. How would you like to do some yoga tomorrow?" Harry asked.

Ensconced in my comfortable corner, I moved not a muscle.

"It's not a question, Randolph," Harry said sharply. "It's a command. I'm getting tired of hearing this fat jazz. Three people mentioned it on the street tonight. Three! It's time we did a bit of work."

By "we," my owner meant *me.* Of course, if Harry had been genuinely concerned, he would have refrained from piling the spareribs on my plate that evening.

"Remember we're having lunch at Jackson's tomorrow, which gives us the morning to do our yoga."

Jackson's was a welcome destination, I only wished we could detour around yoga to get there. After Harry went to bed, I climbed onto a chair next to the kitchen table to survey the messages. I didn't have anything else to communicate to Harry for now but I cleared a small space and began to assemble Imogen's code:

$_{12}$*CDYZMNBCEFLMIJNOEF8$_9$.* Trying to decipher the code in my head had been pointless and I thought it might be good to see it in front of me. This had one immediate result: the numbers dropped out because Alpha-Bits, of course, do not have numbers. I realized that the numbers had been a distraction. In all likelihood they were not central to the code at all. They were more like bookends to the actual message. I stared at *CDYZMNBCEFLMIJNOEF* for an hour or so. A few times it seemed like a solution was about to appear, but it never did. Then I too went to bed.

At nine the next morning with sleep still heavy upon me, we boarded the subway as guide dog and blind owner (our ruse had obvious usefulness) and soon arrived at the Pooch Palace — Canine Pool and Spa. A yoga class had already begun. I was led by a trim, athletic-looking girl to a mat. The mat was one of six positioned in front of a mirror. Owners were to remain with their dogs and assist them as they stretched and posed. Yours Truly had no trouble with the first pose, *Downward Dog,* which seemed custom-made for my physique. The same could not be said for *Twisted Serpent* or *Springing Lion,* both of which savaged my back and hindquarters. The torture continued with *Crooked Root* and *Bulbous Frog.* If I resisted the instructor's manipulations, my limbs would be yanked into conformity. The session concluded with *Soft Belly.* I excelled at

Soft Belly.

"Harry?" A shrill female voice shattered my yoga calm.

Two identical-looking blond women stood in the entrance to the yoga room. A tragically coiffed standard white poodle stood between them. One of the women was Belinda, the owner of the "haunted" house in New Jersey that Harry and Ivan had "exorcised." Harry, who was following along with dog yoga, shut his eyes and breathed into a final stretch. His feigned absorption was no match for Belinda who seemed incapable of understanding that she was being ignored.

"Whatever you two did, it worked. We haven't had a problem since."

I recognized the other woman as Zest Kilpatrick, the news reporter from the night before whose reckless television feature had caused me to endure such inhumane activity that morning.

"Glad to hear it," Harry said. "It doesn't always work."

"Well, it did this time. And I don't mind air-drying some of my lingerie — it's amazing the hardships you can learn to live with."

"Hardships, right," Harry managed.

"I am so happy that you're here. I've been telling my friend Zest about you. She's the one I said was in entertainment."

The reporter stepped forward and shook Harry's hand.

"Zest Kilpatrick for *Channel 8 — News on the Eight.*"

"Isn't that news, not entertainment?" Harry objected.

"News *is* entertainment these days," Zest said. "We give our viewers what they want. Life is heavy enough."

"We came down because of your story," Harry said.

"The power of the local news," Zest said. "Channel 8 reaches 1.2 million households in the tristate area. I'm sorry, 1.275 million households."

"And even more by satellite, isn't that right, Zest?" Belinda asked.

"We're saturating the planet."

Harry collected our things and snapped the leash onto my collar. He looked me in the eyes.

"How are you doing, buddy? Spirit of the universe buzzing through your veins?"

I could only have wished for such a pleasant outcome from my exertions. Instead, the spirit of the universe was making itself known in different ways: joints and muscles seemed to have been replaced by sandpaper and hot tar, my eyeballs throbbed, even my tail hurt.

The women dissected Harry in the third person.

"The chin."

"The chin is awesome."

"And the eyes . . ."

"Totally awesome."

"If you'd excuse me," Harry said. "I've got a lunch date."

"Hard to get," Zest said.

"Very," Belinda said.

My owner had had enough.

"I'm not playing hard to get," Harry said. "I'm already got."

"He's taken," Zest groaned. "You didn't tell me he was taken."

"There's no such thing," Belinda said. "What guys really mean is that they're waiting for the right girl to come around and take them."

"No," Harry said. "I mean I'm taken. The right girl already came around and she took me."

"Where is she?" Belinda asked. "I wouldn't let you out of my sight if I were her."

Harry began to walk up the stairs.

"I'm flattered that you like me and think that I'm worth anybody's trouble, but really I'm not."

"Humble too," Belinda said.

"Belinda, we're embarrassing ourselves," Zest said.

The television reporter's boy-crazy hyperbole had suddenly disappeared and was replaced by politeness.

"Well, it was nice meeting you. I hope you weren't too offended," Zest said. "You know how us girls get sometimes."

Harry said he understood.

"Thanks for watching Channel 8."

Harry and I kept walking.

"Wait," Zest said. "Please wait."

She caught up with us.

"If you ever need anything — you have a tip on a story or something, who knows — here's my card."

Zest tucked the business card into Harry's shirt pocket and gave it a pat.

"No hard feelings?"

"Sure."

"People are always telling me that I come on too strong. It's good for TV but it stinks with my love life."

"Don't worry about it," Harry said.

"You know you look really familiar," Zest said. Then she frowned and looked downcast as she remembered. "Oh, the girl . . . I'm so sorry . . ."

"I was on television a lot then," Harry said.

When we got outside, my owner decided he wanted to walk the many blocks to Jackson's. Broken in body though I was, I did not resist. Harry needed some air.

A Dog Arrives in
One Piece
Jackson Tells a Tale

Jackson met Harry at the door with a drink.

"What's wrong with Randolph?" Jackson asked.

"Nothing," Harry said.

"Nothing?" Jackson protested. "The animal can barely walk."

Having dragged his dog almost fifty blocks, my owner only now noticed my alarming condition.

"I guess that's from the yoga. He'll get used to it."

I shook my whole body. This is a gesture among dogs that is universally misinterpreted by humans. After a dog has had a tiff with another dog or has been frightened, upset or disturbed in some other way, you will notice the animal shake himself vigorously from head to tail. The dog is ridding himself of any feelings of social confusion and distress. In humans this animal tendency has been confined to the much less satisfying shake of the head, shrug of the shoulders or lifting of both hands and arms skyward. Why man lost this great stress-relieving full body shake that his earlier evolutionary versions undoubtedly possessed is a mystery. Certainly none of these other gestures do much to help get rid of the resentment and petty slights that can crush and disfigure the personality and deaden the spirit. Nothing Harry said would offend me for long. Yes, with a good shake, one could move on to lunch.

Jackson led Harry to the sofa, navigating major and minor mountains of clutter all of which seemed to have grown since our last visit. Lunch — catered tea sandwiches and a host of finger foods waiting on the sideboard — would be preceded by the venerable custom of a drink and conversation.

Everything seemed the same, yet everything was changed. I struggled to see Jackson as I once had. But instead of our generous, kind and educated friend, I couldn't rid my mind of the Marlin-witnessed images: the secretive man appearing in the apartment in a strange outfit; the violent man pushing Beatrice against a bookcase. I wanted to reach Marlin, but I could barely see the tree sloth let alone approach him — piles of books and a newly acquired mannequin cut off all paths to his tree and only his back peaked out from behind the drapes.

"The lawsuit continues," Jackson told Harry. "The little scholar refuses to give up. He says he will not stop until he makes me pay one way or another either through cash or an apology or both. But I shall prevail."

Harry asked about Jackson's health. This resulted in an avalanche of information on the latest treatments for aging. Jackson didn't think that aging was something one just accepted. He had enrolled in an Alzheimer's study that measured the effect of mental exercise on the development of the condition. He was required to do the *New York Times* crossword puzzle every day (which he did anyway) and keep a log of everything he read.

"Aging is a disease for which we have no cure . . . only painkillers," Jackson insisted.

He poured more sherry into Harry's glass. "We're not meant to break down like this. Few people see it that way, because aging has been with us for so long. But that doesn't stop it from being a disease. They're doing experiments with worms. They've isolated a gene. Instead of having a two-week lifespan, the worm ends up living four weeks. That's double. Imagine if humans could achieve that: 160 years or so. Wow. Of course, you and I won't benefit from it — they'll have to make the changes in the womb. But there are steps we can take . . ."

"Like giving up cigars," Harry suggested with the rare flicker of a smile.

"Thanks for the reminder. I have two Cubans saved for after lunch."

Our host gestured to the sideboard where a small yellow box stood. Jackson's only hope of locating anything for immediate use seemed to be keeping it in one place, like this small yellow box, an easily found sanctuary among the chaos.

Jackson asked if Harry was hungry. Harry nodded and soon everyone, including Yours Truly, was eating the tea sandwiches. Later the cigars were brought out and great clouds of blue gray smoke filled the suite.

"And you, young man? How is the New Year treating you?"

Jackson stretched his legs out in front of him and toppled a pile of books and magazines in the process.

"Strangely," Harry muttered.

"Strangely?"

Jackson leaned toward my owner.

Harry told Jackson about his experiences with Iris, Beatrice and Michael. He spoke about their strange conversations, the possibility of foul play and the plummeting air conditioner. Then my owner mentioned how Overton might have been electrocuted.

Jackson's coolness instantly disappeared. In its place was something I never expected to see: a desperate need. The sudden change of scent was unmistakable. Jackson had always seemed like one of those benevolent guardians in a Dickens novel, supporting everyone from behind the scenes and never needing anything himself. But now Jackson needed something . . . I couldn't tell exactly what, but it was powerful.

Jackson jumped to his feet and then sat back down again. He drummed his fingers on the sofa nervously. He bit his lip. Then he fixed his eyes on my owner and began to speak in hushed, confidential tones.

"Harry, I've got something important to tell you, but before I tell you I need you to promise that you won't tell anyone."

My owner promised.

"I know that I must seem like an eccentric sort of a man, living like this. By accident of birth I have more money than any single person should ever be responsible for — and believe me it is a responsibility. Every day it takes a few hundred people to go to work — hard, backbreaking work — to earn less money collectively than my money earns in interest in the first few minutes of the morning. Money is their motive for leaving their beds, their wives, their children, walking out the door and going somewhere they don't want to go so they can keep everything that they have to leave every day.

"Money has never been like that for me, but it has been a responsibility. I'm aware that in some cosmic equation, I have to give back, and I do. I've made arrangements that upon my death everything goes to worthy hands, but that's not what I want to talk about now. Money is a responsibility in another way as well. It makes one a custodian of a kind of trust. I'm not the ideal candidate for this kind of trust, because I am by nature a theoretical sort of person. I don't like to act; I like to think. If I liked to act, this apartment wouldn't be smothered in a knee-high pile of things that I can't bear to throw away."

Jackson exhaled a large cloud of cigar smoke and watched it hang in the early afternoon light.

"Vultures, Harry. That's really what I'm talking about. When you have a great deal of money you encounter the worst things in human beings and the worst kind of people. I have spent my life fending off advances from the big-idea men, the venture capitalists, the players of all stripes."

"You've always been generous with me," Harry said.

"Because you never asked me to be generous but you needed it more than any of them. A genuine artist gives of himself and never thinks of the cost. You are the real thing. The people I'm talking about are nothing like that. They want an easy life. For some reason they think they deserve something that no one on this planet deserves and something the vast majority of people can't even find no matter how hard they try.

"The old man in front of you has more than a few secrets," Jackson said. "Now this is where your promise matters."

Harry nodded.

"I have been in love with Iris for over four decades," Jackson said.

"What?" Harry sounded shocked.

"You probably thought I was the standard, wealthy aesthete — urbane, witty, probably gay. No. I'm the unconventional heterosexual male who could never forget his first love, could never move on, could never succeed in loving someone else, who finally accepted the position of loving at a distance."

Harry gazed out the window thoughtfully.

"Not much of a physical distance, I know. But she might as well have lived on the other side of the world. Iris would never have anything to do with me."

"Is that why you live here?" Harry asked. "To be near her."

Jackson punched the air with his cigar.

"No. That is why she lives *there*."

He stood up again and stretched.

"I own that apartment and I have been paying her taxes, her co-op fees and her utilities for decades. It's all very strange and convoluted. We don't ever meet in person or talk on the telephone. All of the apartment-related mail goes to me. If on occasion I need to get a message to her I do so in written form through the doorman of the building; she does the same in my case through the Belvedere's concierge."

"I had no idea."

"Harry, if someone really loves, he loves her as he finds her. If he doesn't like what he finds that doesn't mean that love ceases to exist or that the same love can be packed away and applied to someone else."

"But it was you who had her live across the street."

"Of course, that is what it would look like to you, but I never had her do anything that she didn't want to do. There were never any strings attached. When she took the apartment, we were good friends. I was in love with her but I hadn't told her my feelings. I was traveling a lot then, and when I was in New York I would stay at this hotel. At the end of a boozy night, we were standing by that window over there and she looked out and noticed the apartment."

Jackson gestured at the window.

"The owner was in the process of moving out. The carpets were rolled up, half the books were in packing boxes and the sofa disassembled. She said she would love to live there because she'd be able to see me right across the street whenever I was in New York, and when I wasn't in New York she could look down the street and see Central Park. I thought this was a grand idea and with all the conviction and energy of a head full of champagne, we marched across the street to the building, found the owner and bought the apartment."

"Then things changed?" Harry prodded.

"You know, Harry, when I was a child — even when I became a young man, I used to look at all the strange adult arrangements, all the permanent sorts of messes people seem to get themselves into — the ex-wives, the children whose dads can't visit, the parents who won't speak to their children and the children who won't speak to their parents. I used to think, How does one end up there? How do you end up where the daily reality of your life is absurd or tragic or so damn well twisted that the normal things in it are like a mockery to anything decent or pleasant or good? And being young I said that would never happen to me. But then it did happen, just like it does to everybody. It's never exactly what happens to everyone else, it's always custom fit. Custom fit to our own strengths, our own weaknesses and our own individual vanities . . . And wonder of wonders you not only learn to live with the mess, you become attached to it. The mess becomes your whole life.

"When I bought that apartment for Iris, did I think that twenty-eight years later I would still be living in this suite without her and that my only contact with her would be through the occasional business note? Absolutely not. Or that I would have become so disciplined at respecting her privacy that I never look out that window anymore?"

"So what happened?"

"You mean how did I go from one boozy night to this?"

Harry nodded.

"I made the mistake of telling her that I loved her."

Jackson relit his cigar.

"Iris said she wanted no pretenses. She could never see me as more than a friend and I could never see her as anything but a love. In her mind that meant that we could have no contact."

"Why did you let her stay?"

"She has an artistic temperament. She wanted certain things, but she was hopeless in getting them. She was attached to the apartment. If I am guilty of one thing, it is allowing her to stay there and accept my support. But she would have been homeless without me."

"And Overton?"

Jackson sat and then stood and then sat back down again.

"He was part of the problem, wasn't he?" he said. "I was in love. I'm still in love. Where Iris is concerned I can't see too clearly. A note of hers about a radiator leak could end with *affectionately yours* and I would spin for weeks, imagining a romantic breakthrough. If she forgot to punctuate, I would see something in that. It was hope that got me here. Hope that she would cross that street one day and say that she was mine. Hope that she was keeping an eye on me for all those years. But as time went on, I began to accept that she was indifferent. I moved into my benevolent protector stage.

Helping when I heard she needed extra help. Medical expenses. That sort of thing. But, remember, never, *ever,* seeing her in person. Then recently I became more active, because I believed that for the first time in her life Iris was in genuine danger."

"From Overton?"

"He wasn't any threat that Iris couldn't deal with. As the years have passed I have come to see Iris for what she is: a distinct type. Of course, all my impressions are built on memories of her in her twenties. Still, I believe she's a fluttering, vague sort of thing, wary of commitment, a hit-and-run lover, and always the delicate artiste, but the delicacy and the flutter and the vagueness — these things are on the surface, these are just the persona. The person is quite different. She told me that her father was one of the best legal minds of his generation — and I imagine that his mind is clicking away somewhere inside her skull beneath all the fluff and blather."

"What do you mean by a type?"

"The longer you live you'll see people fall into these categories. You'll see past their words, their faces, their actions. You'll know what they're capable of and what they could never achieve. I used to think that it was my own prejudice or laziness or blindness that made me label people — and sometimes it might have been — but more often it's because the new person I encounter matches up with some memory, some assessment of a person, or an amalgam of people I met long ago. I may have forgotten the context. I may even have forgotten the exact memory, but it informs how I see the person in front of me. This is harder to do with love. It takes years to separate the emotion from the facts, but I see Iris more for what she is now. That doesn't mean I've stopped loving her or that I think very straight when it comes to her. I just know that she's not so vague."

"I saw a little bit of that at the séance just before Overton died," Harry said.

"You did?"

"She seemed like a nag, and then when I met her again, she was the vague sort of person you're talking about."

"Who was she nagging?"

Jackson's eyes narrowed into a wince. Harry realized that perhaps he had said too much.

"Was it Overton?" Jackson asked.

"Yes," Harry said.

"I think she loved him," Jackson said in a defeated tone.

The ash on his cigar had reached a critical point, but before it broke off and crumbled into the carpet, Jackson tapped it onto his plate next to the remains of his lunch.

Jackon Reveals the Threat
A Grim Phone Call
is Received

The drape inflated in the cold air that blew through the open window and I thought I heard Marlin move about in his tree. For some reason he preferred to stay out of sight. I hoped this meant that the immediate threat had subsided, but doubted it.

"The danger wasn't from Overton," Jackson continued. "It was from letting Beatrice into her life."

"Beatrice?"

"That's not even her name. That's just what she's calling herself now."

"What do you mean?"

"She's gone by many names, our Beatrice."

"She's some kind of con artist?" Harry asked.

"Not some kind, my boy. The classic kind. We forget what the abbreviation stands for: confidence. She is an expert at gaining people's confidence, of weaving herself into their lives, of learning their secrets and gaining their trust. Where did you meet her by the way?"

"At the dog run."

"Walking somebody else's dog, no doubt. She's done that on and off for years."

"You mean she doesn't own a dog?"

"I wouldn't know where she'd keep it. I doubt she has her own apartment."

"How do you know so much about her, Jackson?" Harry asked the question his dog yearned to pose.

Jackson laughed.

"Iris has had a maid for years. A wonderful woman called Fanny who comes six days a week to cook, clean . . ."

"And you pay her," Harry concluded smugly.

"I pay her salary, yes. But there are no strings attached. I had never availed myself of Fanny's services as a spy until I began to sense trouble. Mind you, Fanny would never have spoken to me if she had thought Iris could have protected herself. She's absolutely devoted to Iris. Just after Thanksgiving there was a note waiting for me at the concierge. Fanny wanted to meet at one of those chain coffee places. Abysmal with all that faux world art and repackaged West Coast culture — I'm afraid it's the way of life these days . . .

"Anyway, I drank something posing as espresso and Fanny talked. She was very worried. She said that Beatrice had been hanging around the apartment for months, and one day Fanny had overheard her on the telephone. Beatrice was talking to someone about some kind of plan. Iris was involved. Overton was the target."

"That sounds crazy," Harry said.

"It *is* crazy. I did some research into Beatrice and learned a lot about her. She likes fine art and the old men who own it. She's parted several from their prized possessions — gifts given outright in contemplation of marriage. But she wasn't the marrying kind and after the sale of a piece and the collection of the funds, she invariably disappeared. And so many different names: Victoria Frank, Marjory Adams, Carmen Vallejo and once as Contessa Maria Como, during a conference hosted by a college history department that featured the descendants of the Hapsburgs. Neither the contessa nor her ancestors, mind you, will ever be found in the *Almanach de Gotha,* but our Beatrice is quite a talker. Some enterprising young journalist actually managed to make a documentary about her. Eventually she was caught and charged with some variation of fraud, but she never served time."

Jackson stood up again. I had been keeping careful tabs on his scent. The initial desperation remained but it was joined by more ambiguous smells that I could not quite decipher. It was not at all clear to me how much of what Jackson was telling Harry was the absolute truth or a distortion. It is rare for my nose to be confounded by other smells but the potent contraband Havana cigars seemed to have stunned my olfactories.

"I knew that I couldn't approach Iris directly," Jackson continued. "After so many years, the distance between us had hardened into an inflexible law. I couldn't imagine violating it and besides she would have misunderstood my intentions. But I could monitor things through Fanny, which I did, and I knew I could always approach Beatrice, if I really had to. A few days before Overton's death, I did just that. Fanny had met me again for coffee and told me that Beatrice had been spending a great deal of time at Iris's and her communications by telephone were growing more urgent. There was something that Overton had that Beatrice wanted and somehow she was going to use Iris to get to him. It was vague — Fannie's English is far from flawless — but I decided I had no choice but to confront Beatrice."

"You weren't afraid that word would get back to Iris?"

"Beatrice wouldn't dare speak to Iris if I told her the things I knew. I buttonholed her on the street. To my surprise, she already knew who I was. Iris had talked to her about how a certain man had supported her all these years. Beatrice suggested that Iris was considering ending our financial arrangement. In return, I told her some of the things I knew and I warned her that if anything happened I would hold her responsible."

"How did she react?"

"Beatrice couldn't have been cooler. She admitted nothing. She said that Iris deserved a friend and that men were too controlling. Then she turned on her heel and marched off and I was left standing there worried that Fanny would pay for the confrontation. I was right. A few days later, Iris let Fanny go. I'm still paying her salary, but she's devastated."

"So Beatrice talked her out of the house?" Harry concluded.

"And a few days later Overton was dead," Jackson said.

"And you think Beatrice killed him?"

"I have no proof."

"But you think she did?"

"She's a very clever woman."

Jackson jammed out the cigar on the plate and drew lines in ash across its surface.

"It's so much more complicated than what I've told you so far."

Then the phone rang. It was grim news.

Details of a
Second Curious
Death
Jackson Reflects
on the Urgency of
Life

John James Audubon's decision to publish four leather-bound, double-elephant-sized volumes of *Birds of America* in 1827 had resulted in two things on this January day: (1) over one hundred complete sets were in the hands of fortunate collectors around the world and (2) a double-elephant-sized volume opened to a page featuring the great blue heron slipped from its custom-made viewing platform in the private library of a wealthy bibliophile on Fifth Avenue and caused the untimely death of the woman who was crushed beneath it.

Audubon, the legendary naturalist and painter of birds, was born to a French chambermaid and the captain of a merchant ship in Haiti in 1785. Although raised in France he became the image of the American frontiersman, setting up a general store in Kentucky and modeling himself on Daniel Boone. His passion was birds and in the American wilderness he found a living collection to observe, dissect and draw. This passion led to the eventual publication — at great personal cost — of *Birds of America,* a four-volume series that depicted hundreds of birds in watercolor. Audubon was criticized for not classifying the birds according to the scientific norms of the day. He defended his decision by claiming that his intent was to capture the life of birds and to bring the reader on a virtual expedition through the wilds of America.

Audubon captured the way birds flew, perched, nested and walked. He offered exquisite studies of foliage and topography. The pages burst with color and movement. Turning the pages of the watercolor plates was meant to simulate the popular concept of *moving panoramas,* a pre-cinematic activity popular among Audubon's contemporaries.

He was a man living at the beginning of the mass media age and he understood the need for self-promotion. Audubon wanted his paintings to seize the public's imagination. This was the reason for the double-elephant-sized volumes. These mammoth books weighed hundreds of pounds each.

When opened they were as tall and wide as a small sofa. The double-elephant-sized volumes toured to great acclaim. Audubon's reputation was made on both sides of the Atlantic.

"I'll be there in fifteen minutes," Jackson said into the phone.

He stood motionless among the stacks of papers, books and empty glasses.

"Terrible," Jackson muttered.

He looked at Harry. The strong reek of the Cuban cigars had begun to dissipate and my functioning nose became aware that a sharp anxiety now dominated Jackson's scent.

"A friend has just had something awful happen. I must help him. I wish you'd come along."

Harry nodded. "What about Randolph?"

"We can take him and you can go home from there."

We hurried downstairs and the concierge hailed a taxi for us. The driver began to complain about the presence of Yours Truly but Jackson quieted him with the promise of a handsome tip. Our destination lay near the southeastern corner of Central Park. Our driver took the loop. The city was in deep freeze. The Alberta Clipper had settled in for the long haul and temperatures during the day were in the single digits. That morning the weatherman had said that New York's daytime temperature would be colder than the surface of Mars. As the taxi coasted down the near empty loop past a handful of indefatigable joggers, Jackson provided Harry with background.

The man on the other line was named Thomas Lavery. He was someone Jackson had known since prep school. Like Jackson, Lavery loved the fine arts, but unlike Jackson, Lavery was a self-made man who had paid for his education through scholarships, loans and summer jobs. He had established a substantial fortune as a bond trader. All along Lavery was collecting. He collected everything until his tastes began to narrow, at which point he began to focus on rare art books and prints. His Fifth Avenue apartment boasted a two-level library. In this library could be found hundreds of prints, thousands of rare books and the prized double-elephant-sized *Birds of America.*

Jackson told Harry that he had never heard Lavery out of sorts. This was a man, after all, who had climbed Mount Everest on his sixtieth birthday and never missed running the New York City Marathon.

On the phone, Lavery had stammered out his crisis. He had been hosting a female guest. They had breakfasted together and parted soon after: Lavery to work on expanding his collection of Toulouse-Lautrec prints; his female friend to nap. Sometime later, Lavery had wandered into his library and found the woman dead, pinned beneath Audubon's *Birds of America.* Instead of calling the police, Lavery had called Jackson.

"I have a reputation for keeping my head when all about me are losing theirs," Jackson said.

The taxi whipped around the base of the park and headed north to the Seventy-second Street exit and Fifth Avenue.

"Who was the woman?" Harry asked.

"A 'friend,' " Jackson said. "Tom has always had a lot of female friends."

We arrived at Lavery's building a few minutes later. Jackson gave the driver the kind of tip that was certain to push the campaign for dog friendly taxis forward.

The building was one of those grand Fifth Avenue co-ops that offer vast apartments and wonderful views to anyone who can manage to clear the dozens of financial and social hurdles that the management has erected to maintain the status quo. The doorman who opened our cab door was outwardly welcoming, but simultaneously profoundly aloof. He clearly wouldn't endorse the more obvious snobbishness of the Belvedere's concierge.

"We're here to see Thomas Lavery," Jackson said.

The doorman insisted that Lavery be called, but Jackson would have none of it. The powerful sense of entitlement that old money carries won the day. We boarded the elevator before any further objections could be made.

Lavery answered the door. "You put the doorman on his toes. He called in a huff," he said in a grim voice.

My olfactories were overwhelmed by the sharp odor of anxiety, confusion and the subtle, creeping scent of imagined guilt.

Guilt and imagined guilt are quite different. When someone feels guilty for some bad act that he or she has actually committed, the smell is all encompassing and inexpungible. Picture those dollar bills that hide exploding ink capsules and stain the hands of a thief. Guilt is a wretched and inescapable smell.

Imagined guilt is mild. It comes and it goes. Could I have done something different to have prevented x? Did I do something to cause y? Imagined guilt is a restlessness of mind unsupported by bad action. It is man doubting himself in the face of ambiguous circumstances.

Lavery looked Harry and me over as Jackson introduced us and seemed to accept our presence.

"Let me take you there," he said.

"Why didn't you call the police?" Jackson asked.

"I don't know."

"Lavery, that's not good enough," Jackson pressed.

"I tried to move the book," Lavery confessed. "The fall had bent some of the pages. I'm a collector. I did it without thinking. I know you should never move something at a crime scene."

"A crime scene? Not an accident?"

"It must have been. After I found the body, I went to the kitchen. I poured myself a glass of milk. I don't know why, but I needed milk. I heard something move in the pantry. Then I heard a few bottles fall and break. I went to look. The lights went out, the door opened and someone pushed past me. Before I knew what was happening they had run out the kitchen door that opens onto the service stairwell."

"I see," Jackson said. "And did you call the front desk to stop them?"

"No."

Jackson said nothing.

"I know it looks bad, but there wasn't any point," Lavery continued. "That stairway leads to the back of the building. No one would have been able to stop him."

"Him?" Jackson asked.

"Or her for all I know," Lavery said. "God, this is awful."

"Try not to worry. It will be okay," Jackson assured him. Indeed, my nose told me that flustered thinking and nerves aside, Thomas Lavery was telling the truth about everything.

We reached the library entrance. Two massive mahogany doors intricately carved and polished stood open. It was a magnificent space, astounding gilt bindings row on row wrapping around Beaux Arts shelves and lit by the crystal blossom of an enormous chandelier — but for the moment my focus was on something in the center of the room. A woman's legs protruded from beneath the largest book I had ever seen.

I immediately recognized something familiar about the body. Very familiar. The corpse wore Beatrice's shoes and the trace of her perfume mingled with the distinct smell of . . .

"Death," Jackson announced.

"I think she's been dead for hours," Lavery said.

"Where were you?"

"I told you," Lavery said. "I was negotiating with some guy in Dubai for a new Lautrec. I saw her face. It's horrible."

"Tom, go call the police."

"Are you certain, Jack?" Lavery asked.

"I'm certain. Once you've done that why don't you go to the kitchen and have another glass of milk."

"Should I call my lawyer?"

"There's no need right now."

Lavery departed and we were left with the body. Neither Harry nor Jackson recognized Beatrice yet and they kept their distance from the corpse.

"Poor woman," Harry said.

I tried to pull my owner toward her, but he resisted.

"No, Randolph," Harry objected. "No."

He yanked my leash.

"Sit."

Unpleasant job though it would be, I had to get a good noseful of the crime scene. Lavery was not involved in Beatrice's murder — I felt certain of that. The most obvious suspect was Michael, but beneath the mingling of perfume and death in the air, I could detect no trace of his scent. I had to get closer to the body before the authorities arrived. Harry and Jackson, in an effort to distract themselves, began to discuss Lavery's collection of prints.

"Tom owns almost a third of all the Lautrecs outside the major collections," Jackson said.

He pointed out the framed prints and posters that occupied portions of the non-shelved walls.

"They're amazing," Harry said.

"Aren't they? Every time I see a Lautrec, something happens right here." Jackson tapped his chest. "It's like the arrival of spring."

Harry approached a poster for the Folies-Bergère and traced the leg of a showgirl with his finger.

"Weightless," Harry said. "It's like a cloud painted on a cloud."

"The poor little drunken midget had a gift."

"And he used it," Harry added.

"Despite tragedy, opposition, scorn," Jackson philosophized. "We have this brief window to do something against the odds of our existence. Then the window closes. The talented midget drinks himself to death; the woman dies under a double-elephant-sized volume filled with pictures of birds."

They moved on to another Lautrec.

"What's Randolph doing?" Jackson asked with a note of concern in his voice.

"Randolph, don't!" Harry shouted. "Come back here."

But it was too late. Harry had let my leash go slack and I took advantage of this to perform my emergency Houdini maneuver, puffing up my neck and then contracting repeatedly, which enabled me to slip from my collar. I might be more than a few jogs short of prime physical condition but my four Labrador legs are still superior to my owner's two in a sprint. In an instant I had crossed the floor and reached Beatrice's body careful not to get too close — I didn't want to disturb the crime scene and corrupt any forensic investigation. But I got close enough to fill my olfactories with a generous sample. Suddenly my head spun with a myriad of scents: Beatrice's perfume, her fear, her confusion, her anger and the onset of physical decay. The former Kwo Bo expert and con artist had been terrified as she died, but also confused. The confusion suggested a surprise of some kind, but I could not fathom what it was.

I did not resist as Harry snapped my collar around my neck and pulled me back to the edge of the room like a common criminal. I had my data.

"Bad dog," he said.

Just then Lavery appeared with the police. The authorities told Harry to remove me and I was promptly taken to an adjacent room.

"I'm very disappointed in you, Randolph," Harry said grimly as he closed the door.

I found myself in a small study with a rug, a few chairs and a large television. I could hear none of what was unfolding in the library so I stretched out and began to sift through the data, an abundance of contradictory scents. Hours prior to her death, perhaps over breakfast with Lavery, she and her host had luxuriated in the groves of Eros. How little our Beatrice had resembled Dante's chaste lady of whom the poet sang: *She is one worthier than I.* Our Beatrice liked her men and apparently even more so after a hearty breakfast.

Half an hour or more passed and I arrived at a conclusion. I had assembled a record of her final day — or, rather, half-day — and there was no trace of Michael in any of it.

Harry opened the door.

"They're kicking us out," he said.

My owner looked shaken. He had obviously learned the identity of the corpse.

Jackson had been permitted to stay while two detectives had taken Lavery to a far room for questioning, but they wanted Harry to leave. The library was now abuzz with men and women in jumpsuits and uniforms. Beatrice had not been moved, but the book had been taken away and a photographer was snapping pictures. Her face was the color of a blood sausage. She rested on her back with her upward facing palms at her side, open and calm, as if she were taking a nap in an odd place.

A Chase Through Central Park The Virtue of Wearing No Pants and Having a Large Bladder

A wind blew down Fifth Avenue with a bite that cut through my well-insulated coat and caused my owner to shout in pain.

"My God, that's cold."

Harry wanted to take a taxi, but found that he had left his money at home.

On any other day, a walk would be something of a treat. We could make our way into Central Park, the wonderful rustic vision of Frederick Law Olmsted and Calvert Vaux, wind our way past the Wollman ice rink, up through the dairy, down the poet's walk to the bandstand, the Bethesda Terrace, the boathouse and then over to Imogen's favorite, the bronze statue of Alice perched atop a Wonderland mushroom. But given the subzero reality of the Alberta Clipper, we seemed to be setting out on a doomed mission — an absurd Manhattan reenactment of Shackleton's quest for the South Pole. I hoped that Harry and I would not die frozen in a snowbank.

Nevertheless, we set out on foot up Fifth Avenue, walking straight into the wind. Traffic lights heaved back and forth, awnings whipped and trees bent. We entered the park at Seventy-second Street.

Harry knew Central Park very well. When Imogen was with us, we had spent hours wandering its 843 acres. How many picnics on the Great Lawn and operas in the park we had relished, I could not count. And in happier days, Harry had covered forty miles a week running its roads and trails as he prepared his cardiovascular system for the annual masochism of the New York City Marathon.

Central Park is modeled on an English garden. An English garden resists easy navigation. It is impossible in Central Park to walk in a straight line on the major paths between a southeastern point and a northwestern one. My owner sought the most direct route home. To do this we would have to go off road.

"We'll take the Ramble," Harry shouted over the wind.

In the Ramble the park's designers had created a faux American wilderness complete with limestone outcroppings, winding paths, sudden vistas, streams and narrow footbridges. Even on warm days the Ramble is less populated than most of the park. In this weather it would be deserted.

Harry and I passed the boathouse restaurant. Brunch was long over, dinner was an hour away and no one was around. We crossed a small parking lot that held an empty tour bus and several official park trucks. The sun was setting and the woods were filling with darkness.

Perhaps it was seeing Beatrice's body, but I felt nervous and weak. Sudden movement on an oak's lower branches made me stiffen with fear until I realized it was a squirrel. A shrub along the path shook. I jumped only to see three grackles take flight.

"I know how you feel," Harry said.

We slipped into the Ramble and soon we were out of sight of the road. The trees reduced the wind but they also cut the light.

"At least it isn't as cold here," Harry observed.

My owner began to jog, but his out of shape animal soon forced him to assume a more reasonable pace. Soon we were in the middle of the Ramble. It was impossible to hear anything but the wind and the crisp sound of our feet in the ice and snow. We were profoundly alone in the heart of a city of eight million souls.

Then I smelled Michael. At first I thought it was just a residual scent, some strange confluence of odor lingering in my fur or on the hem of Harry's trousers mixing with and being amplified by an overactive imagination. Perhaps it was memory, I thought, scent memory (I had experienced this kind of thing before).

But this was different. Those smells had disappeared abruptly and did not return. Michael's smell came to me in waves that corresponded with the wind, which now blew in gusts from the north. With each new gust I smelled Michael. He smelled very anxious, very angry and very determined. The scent was growing more powerful and we seemed to be walking in his direction.

I planted my feet and endured the unpleasant snap of the collar around my neck as my owner came to a sudden stop.

"*Now* what's wrong?" Harry asked.

The road forked ten feet in front of us. One path veered off into an even darker thicket of trees and disappeared around a mound of rocks. The other path led straight ahead. Somewhere up this second path Michael was waiting for us.

"Come on, Randolph. This is ridiculous.

If we keep walking we'll be home in fifteen minutes."

I began to walk, but when we reached the fork, I pulled hard to the left.

"No you don't," Harry objected.

He pulled back on the leash.

"We're going straight. I have no idea where that other path leads, and I'm not going to find out in this weather."

But I kept pulling to the left.

"Go straight and I'll order Chinese as soon as we get home," Harry implored.

But I would not be bribed and finally my owner relented.

"You can forget the Chinese," he said.

We made our way around the jumble of rocks.

"In fact, you can forget dinner altogether."

The straight line Harry had wanted to follow had become hopelessly tangled. We went down a flight of stairs, through a narrow tunnel-like passageway, emerged on an open path, crossed a stream and went in a wide arc around the western section of the boathouse lake. Every so often, the lights of the Dakota, the San Remo and a snatch of the Natural History Museum were visible through gaps in the trees. They looked very far away.

Michael's scent vanished. I had almost

begun to relax when fifty feet behind us a rock bounced off another rock, rolled down the hill and struck the hollow trunk of a dead tree.

Harry quickened his pace.

"Ten minutes and we're home."

The wind, which had been blowing from the front, shifted and began to blow from behind us and once again I smelled Michael. He was closing the gap. I began to pull Harry forward. He didn't resist. We sped past trees and up a short incline. I caught a glimpse of the Belvedere Castle through a gap in the foliage and pulled even harder.

"Stop," a male voice said from behind us.

It was Michael.

Harry and I kept moving.

"Stop, dammit."

"It's Michael," Harry hissed.

"Don't make me run," Michael insisted.

Harry wrapped my leash tightly around his right hand, and we began to sprint up the hill toward the castle. The tea sandwiches in my stomach prepared to evacuate. I swore that I would begin a routine of regular exercise, if and when this crisis came to a happy conclusion.

Michael pounded up the hill after us. He was in good shape for an expert on the decorative arts. We rounded a corner and found our way blocked by a chain-link fence. We had reached the border of one of the several sunken streets that carry motor traffic across the park. There are only a few ways over the roadway at Seventy-ninth Street. Our path, unfortunately, wasn't one of them.

Harry reached down, scooped Yours Truly up and threw me over the fence. Then he vaulted it himself. We were well down the fence line when Michael began to climb.

"I think we're good," Harry said.

We jumped the fence again when we reached the path that crossed Eighty-sixth Street. Harry hurried me up the hill and we arrived at Belvedere Castle. We crossed the empty pavilion. There wasn't a single human being in sight.

"He's got to be well behind us now," Harry speculated.

Just as my owner said this, Michael stepped out of the shadows.

"This is silly," Michael said, trying to catch his breath. "It's just me. I met you at Iris's. Why are you running away?"

Night had fallen, and we stood in separate spheres of light, some distance apart.

"I need to talk to you," Michael gasped.

The Great Lawn stretched to the north

circled by lamplights so far away that they seemed part of a constellation. The wind buffeted the stones of the castle. The loop was hundreds of yards distant, cut off by woods and a precipice that fell into an ice-thatched pond.

We were near the flight of stairs that lead toward the Shakespeare Garden and the Delacorte Theater. The stairs are made of stone and quite steep.

Michael began to walk toward us.

"I'm harmless," Michael said. "This is stupid. I just want to show you something."

He reached into his pocket, but Harry didn't wait to find out what it was.

He disconnected my leash and started to run. He leaped down the stairs three at a time, stumbled on the middle landing but kept going. I tried to stay with him, but dogs are better at running up stairs than down and I lagged far behind my owner. Michael had not anticipated that we would continue to run and did not follow us right away. This gave us a decent lead.

Harry cleared the last step. He was limping. The stumble had taken its toll. Harry would never be able to outpace Michael in this state. But I had a plan.

I had once caused my owner some embarrassment when during a previous winter I had done a Number 1 on the pavement in front of our building (a rare urgency had overcome my *Foliage-Finder* nature). The liquid had frozen instantly on the cold stone and my owner found himself apologizing to an old woman who had the bad luck of slipping on the resulting ice.

Fortunately, my bladder was now full to bursting. Michael had just begun his descent. I squatted in our pursuer's path. As I delivered my Number 1 at the base of the stairs, I stared up at him defiantly. What I could see of his face made me wonder whether we were in any danger at all. Michael looked frustrated and a little amused. He certainly did not appear sinister, but, then again, how many killers do? Some are so divorced from the basic values of life that inflicting death with a smile is nothing more than an ironic gesture.

When Michael reached the landing where Harry had fallen a moment before, the hint of amusement had become a grin. What could be so funny? Then I realized what he was staring at: me.

He did not see a stalwart warrior, a grim-faced defender blocking his way. My face is incapable of such a range of expressions. He saw a dog with big brown eyes looking dreamily up the stairs and urinating on the path.

When Michael was just a few steps away, I finished. He caught sight of Harry turning the corner that led downhill to the Delacorte Theater and picked up his pace.

This was a grave error. The base of the stairs had frozen just as I hoped. The moment he stepped onto the ice Michael lost his footing. His right leg slipped up into space. His left leg struggled to keep him upright, but his momentum carried him forward while gravity forced him down. He collapsed into a heap at the base of the steps.

Yours Truly did not stick around, but as I turned the corner after Harry, I looked back. Michael was not badly injured, but the chase was over. He tried to stand up, but cried out when he put pressure on his left foot. The object that he had held in his hand had fallen to the ground with him. It was no weapon after all, but a packet of photographs that had opened and were now scattered around him on the ground.

"Randolph, we have got to get you into shape. You took forever," Harry told me when I had finally caught up with him.

Soon we had exited Central Park and were walking up the well-lit sidewalk in the company of passersby and the security of doorman-watched buildings.

"Dogs are supposed to run. I didn't see any teeth bared either. What about a bark? Why don't you ever bark?"

I did not dignify his comments with a response. Barking and wagging my tail are activities I do sparingly. Besides I was aware of the distinguished service I had just performed.

Our apartment was warm. There was a message from Jackson on the answering machine. The police did not suspect Lavery. There had been some development that Jackson said he could not go into over the phone but needed to speak to Harry about urgently.

Harry tried Jackson's number but no one answered.

My owner ordered Chinese, but when the food arrived he restricted me to a single sparerib, half an egg roll and a slice of scallion pancake.

"It's for your own good," he insisted.

This was dismal. The little gray cells — so in need of energy — could have used a good feed.

Harry paced the apartment while he ate, leaving a trail of Chinese food across the floor. He looked out the window, bent down to pick up clothes only to let them fall back again and then finally he paused before his unfinished portrait of Imogen. He stared at it as he had done so many times as if there was so much that he needed to tell her. He lifted the engagement ring off his neck and clasped it tightly in his large hand. Then he turned away and settled down into the La-Z-Boy and watched a so-called reality television show. College coeds competed to see how many cockroaches they could eat in a minute.

I nestled into my corner with my back to the television and listened to the wind.

A Dog Has Dreams
A Direction is
Found

I slept fitfully that night. Harry remained in the La-Z-Boy. He seemed anxious and awoke from dozing only to stare at the door as if at any moment Michael might push his way into our apartment. He had propped a kitchen chair under the front doorknob as a stop and hung bells from it to alert us to any intruder.

My dreams were great gushing streams of logic, half-logic and fever-logic. Beatrice appeared and made blood sausages out of fine china and Lautrec paintings. Lavery took dance instruction from a blue heron wearing a tiara. Iris and Michael floated through the visions, specters smoking French cigarettes. Michael proclaimed his innocence; Beatrice her eternal damnation and Jackson a sort of good-hearted bafflement at the proceedings. Phrases from Imogen's journal and fragments of the code ticker-taped across these images: *Family Saga . . . And there are other things too . . . Overton says he fears for his life . . . ZMNBC . . .* All would soon be right; nothing would ever be right. I awoke with a whimper.

"It's okay, Randolph," Harry said. "It was just a dream. You're chasing rabbits again."

But the dreams would not stop. They had tentacles that reached out into our recent history and claimed great chunks of fact only to drag them into the meat grinder of the unconscious and spit them back out wholly changed. The parade of strange images and mad scenarios continued until just before dawn when I awoke again to find that this nocturnal Mardi Gras had borne fruit.

We were afraid of the wrong person. The absence of his scent on Beatrice's body ruled out Michael as her killer. Then there was his plaintive appeal in Central Park. Our first impression and the words of Beatrice, who after all was a con, had blinded us to the actual man. Nothing in his manner suggested harm. Why he was near the apartment where Beatrice was murdered and why he followed us into the park remained important questions, but he had held a sheaf of photographs in his hand not a weapon and he smelled anxious but not threatening. He was desperate to tell us something. I doubted that a murderer would be desperate to tell us anything.

It was vital that we find him and hear what he had to say. I needed to compose another message.

Around five that morning, Harry stumbled out of the La-Z-Boy and into the bedroom. When the door had closed behind my owner, I got to work. The letters had grown a little ratty, my nose was overly damp from our adventure in the cold, but the message was a simple one and I composed it swiftly:

DON'T BE AFRAID OF MICHAEL LISTEN
TO HIM

I settled back down into my corner to await the dawn among the paints and canvases. Reason alone will not save us, especially when the variables include our fellow creatures and their perplexing behaviors — those motives, desires and caprices quite beyond the pale of mere calculation. Fortunately, mind has more than reason, it has the murky, bubbling cauldron of the unconscious spilling out conclusions fully formed that are inevitable and correct but far beyond the ability of conscious thought.

That night's dreams had revealed something important. Sitting in the early morning silence, things became even more clear.

The situation might be a muddle, but now I knew the direction we must go and the assumptions that we had to treat as absolute truth if we were to get anywhere at all: Overton had been murdered. One of two people, not three or four, was the killer: Jackson or Iris. Beatrice had known something that required her death and the person who had killed Overton had killed her. Michael was in the same category as Beatrice. Far from being a threat, he would likely be the next to die.

A Telephone Goes Unanswered A Theory of Murder is Threatened

Harry emerged from his bedroom at nine o'clock that morning. The television reported the departure of the Alberta Clipper and the arrival of above-average temperatures and more wind.

"Crazy weather," he said.

Worried that he would overlook my message, I whimpered at the kitchen table.

"Walk?" Harry asked.

Then he saw it.

"Oh."

He read in silence.

"Persistent thing, our ghost."

Harry sat back down in the La-Z-Boy and began to drum his hand on its well-worn arm. My owner is not jumpy or easy to spook. His body is calm and measured. But the events of the past two weeks — had it only been two weeks? — had caught up with him.

"What do we do?" he asked.

284

My owner tapped the floor with both feet.

"How do we find Michael?"

He threw himself back into the chair.

"Imogen, where are you?"

But the apartment only answered with silence.

I sidled up to Harry. He took no comfort.

"And you — inspired one — what do you suggest we do?"

I hesitated. Then I thought of Jackson and Michael and Iris and Beatrice. Beatrice was in a morgue being poked and prodded, sliced and snipped in a methodical attempt to find a cause. The police, if this indeed was the direction things were going, were starting with an enormous blank. Beatrice had a long history of betrayals and vengeance-seekers behind her. Any investigator would be mired in this material for years, seeking some distinct brushstroke that would complete the picture. I was already far ahead, working with a narrow field. I knew things. I was close to some kind of answer. And, most of all, lives depended on me.

I barked at the phone.

"Call someone?"

I barked.

"Who?"

I moved to the refrigerator where Imogen

had arranged a collage of photographs and magnets. Harry was sloppy in many departments, but he scrupulously guarded what Imogen had once arranged and whenever any part of this creation was disturbed, he would hurriedly restore it. In the middle of the mix, Jackson beamed out at the room from an eight-by-ten glossy taken from the press kit of the Rubens Institute and signed with a flourish.

I knocked Jackson's photo onto the floor with one sweep of my moist nose and put my paw squarely on the picture.

The stare that ensued from my owner was the most uncomfortable of my life. There had been a moment when the proprietor of the pet shop had contemplated selling me to a cosmetics testing facility. Harry's stare of disbelief was even more unsettling. It subverted an entire relationship. It threatened the very order of things.

"You understand me?"

To defuse his wonder and reassert the perception that I was "just an animal," I banged my head into the fridge like an idiot. But rather than have the effect I had hoped, Harry just laughed.

"No need to get frustrated. Your half-wit owner gets it."

Harry continued to stare at me as if I were

some freak. I had the paranoid impression that he might be contemplating some way of exploiting me. This fear was unwarranted — an ancestral holdover, no doubt, from times when my kind was regularly put on the barbecue.

The relationship between owner and dog is a complex one. Genuine love and affection cannot be separated from a sort of Stockholm syndrome, the pressure-cooker affection of captive for captor. Deep in the canine bones is the memory of generations of dogs creeping up to man's campfire and staying at man's whim. When wolf first reached out to *Homo sapiens,* or vice versa, is anyone's guess, but the transition to domestication must have been filled with mutual suspicion, disappointment and slow progress to something that resembles compatibility. I don't mean to denigrate the relationship between our species, but its history has remained untold by my kind. We dogs do not pass on our stories. We are bought and sold. We are deprived of the life of the pack that our lupine forbears traded for life with man. Ancient injuries might heal and seem forgotten, but they live on in our reflexes and responses.

Harry left the La-Z-Boy and called Jackson.

"Jackson," Harry said, "are you there? If you're there, pick up. This is Harry. I need to talk to you as soon as possible. I'm thinking of dropping in this morning. If you're around let me know. If you're not let me know. Or you don't have to . . ."

The answering machine gave Harry a kind of stage fright. It was never easy for him to leave concise phone messages. He kept talking.

"Whatever works for you. If it doesn't, that's fine too. Today would be good. Tomorrow would be good. Not equally as good, but good . . ."

He hung up.

"Very articulate, Harry," my owner muttered. Then he decided to call the concierge. The concierge told Harry that as far as he knew, and he had just done a double shift, Jackson had returned the previous evening, but had not left his suite at all that day.

"Are you sure?" Harry asked.

The concierge informed him that except for a fifteen-minute break during which the superintendent watched the desk, his eyes had been wide open. Mr. Temple had made no appearances other than his arrival. If that were all that was required from the caller, the concierge would appreciate being able to return to work.

My owner tried Jackson's number again. No one answered.

"I really don't like this," Harry said.

The front desk of an establishment like the Belvedere does not lose track of its guests. If they said that Jackson had not left the building then he had not left the building.

Harry paced back and forth. Then he sat back down in the La-Z-Boy and began to smoke his emergency cigarettes one after the other. He flipped through the channels, finally arriving at a program for which I have a particular fondness: *MythBusters.* The show features two ingenious men who vigorously apply scientific method to common beliefs to determine whether the beliefs withstand scrutiny. Can alligators live in New York City sewers? Can you build your own jet pack from plans found on the Internet? Can a man be electrocuted from urinating on the third rail? My ears perked up. This myth was the subject of the current episode that was drawing to a close and about to offer an answer. The hosts had built a mannequin, created a urine stream and charged a third rail. The result: nothing. Their conclusion: the urine stream broke up too much over the distance to the third rail. What could kill dogs would not kill men. My theory regarding Overton was suddenly on shaky ground. It was perhaps not completely dead. After all, I had surmised that a powerful shock would not have been intended in the first place. But the program seemed to conclude that nothing more than a localized electric tingle — certainly not the minimal charge needed to disrupt a pacemaker — would be delivered at any distance more than a few inches. Unless Overton had been kneeling right next to the toilet's lip, it was now improbable that electrocution was the cause.

But I had no time to contemplate this new problem. Harry had put on my leash and was pulling me toward the door. He had decided that we needed to reach Jackson now.

An Adventure
without Breakfast
Jackson is Found

We departed immediately and without breakfast. The meager serving of Chinese food the night before had not held me in good stead. My stomach was achingly empty, but I struggled to rise above it for the sake of our mission.

We rushed down Central Park West and within the space of four blocks I was winded. Harry slowed to a fast walk. Two blocks later my breathing had not improved and my owner was forced to reduce his pace even more.

"Dammit, Randolph," Harry said. "We need to get there now."

I steeled myself and some five minutes later we had arrived at the Belvedere.

We whisked into the lobby and were greeted by the raised eyebrows of the concierge.

"Here for Mr. Temple?"

"Yes."

"He just stepped out."

"He what?"

"Went for a walk," the concierge said. "He said that he was late for an appointment with spring."

"But it's the middle of winter," Harry said.

"I'm just telling you what he said."

"Thanks."

"Dogs aren't allowed in the lobby, sir."

"Do you have any idea when he'll be back?"

"No. But dogs are not allowed in the lobby."

"Could I leave a message for him?"

"I'd have to ask the manager."

"Fine," Harry muttered and we walked out the door.

"What now?" Harry asked.

I tried to pick up Jackson's scent on the sidewalk but to no avail. The Bull Moose Dog Run was only two blocks away. Knowing that it would offer me an opportunity to do my numbers and allow both of us to collect our thoughts, I pulled my owner in that direction.

We arrived to find the enclosure populated by professional dog walkers, two Scotties dressed in matching tartan sweater vests and caps and a dozen huskies shod redundantly in fur-lined boots. As the *Copycat Dumpers* raced to new targets with an enthusiasm entirely unmatched by their imagination, Harry and I made our way across the gravel past a dog barking furiously at anybody who wore a hat.

"He's wearing a hat, Babs," the dog's owner said. "People wear hats."

A posse of dogs threatened to block our passage across the run. My owner, oblivious to the etiquette of my kind, pushed past Kirby, Shelby, Kipling and Tobias as they swooped in for the customary hindquarter sniffs of introduction and information exchange. A few dogs wore plastic cones around their heads. The cones either protected the scars of a recent surgery or passersby from the dog's tendency to bite. A whippet circled around us like a Jet Ski in overdrive. Two fragile-looking women struggled to uncouple their *Little Humper,* a Jack Russell, from a Burmese mountain dog. A *Little Humper* has the perilous habit of taking its chances with the largest dogs in any yard.

Only after Harry had led me to the fence beneath the farthest oak did he remember that there was no need to keep me on my leash. Freed, I sought the relative seclusion offered between the oak's base and the outside fence. After yesterday's high-drama

Number 1, my preferences would be indulged.

I had reached a sort of readiness, when there was an interruption.

"Randolph, it's Daisy Mae," Harry exclaimed.

The Great Dane had arrived. With the customary disregard that big creatures have for small, she had already managed to trample a powder puff wearing a jeweled collar. I half expected to see Beatrice in tow, but her walker was someone I did not recognize.

When Daisy Mae spotted me, she charged. This time, however, just before impact, the woman issued a command in a voice little louder than a whisper. The enormous dog came to an immediate halt and sat down. The woman approached the Great Dane and delivered a brief lecture on proper behavior. Daisy Mae listened with rapt attention.

"I'm afraid she gave yours a fright," the woman said to Harry.

"We're used to it."

"You've met Daisy Mae before?"

Harry nodded.

"I usually have her walked when I'm at work. You probably met one of my people."

Harry nodded again.

"I've always wondered whether they have the same control over her as I do. I doubt it."

"Probably not."

"Harriet might be okay. The other one let Daisy run wild."

"The other one?" Harry asked, knowing what the answer would be.

"She took over when Harriet went to Las Vegas for a week."

"Beatrice?"

"How do you know her?"

"I met her here with your dog."

"She's quite a talker, isn't she?"

"She seemed that way."

The woman's voice dropped. "I don't usually say things against people, but I'm telling dog owners because I think it's important. I got her name from a flyer. Harriet had put me on the spot because she didn't get me a substitute when she went on vacation. I was stupid. I can't prove it, but I'm sure she stole from me. You know how you've got to give dog walkers the keys to your apartment so that they can get your dog during the day when you're not there? I'm more sad than angry about it really. She stole a little broach that my mother gave me just before she died. It had been in our family for generations. I thought I had misplaced it — nothing else in my bedroom was disturbed — but then I put two and two together. By that time she was long gone. I haven't seen her since. Anyway, I just want to let people know so it doesn't happen to them."

"That's too bad."

"You live and learn I guess."

"I guess."

The woman glanced at her watch.

"I'm late for my nutritionist," she said.

She snapped on Daisy Mae's collar.

"She'll get hers in the end," the woman said as she led Daisy Mae across the yard.

"She did," Harry muttered.

I concluded my business. We left the dog run and returned to Jackson's residence for the second time that morning.

"He's here," the concierge announced. "You can go up."

We began to walk to the elevator.

"He's there alright," the concierge continued. "He's just not *all* there if you know what I mean."

Jackson met us at the door. He held a tumbler full of something that looked like Scotch. He was very drunk.

"I'm sorry," he said.

"What for, Jackson?"

"For everything."

He waved the tumbler and spilled half its contents.

"Why don't we sit down?" Harry asked. He took Jackson by the elbow and guided him through the piles of books and papers to the couch.

"You've never seen me like this? It must be a shock. Doesn't happen that much to the old man, but when it does — watch out world, pathetic geriatric sentimentality on its way."

"What happened, Jackson?"

"That woman dead happened."

"It was a shock," Harry said.

Jackson nodded.

"I'm a sensitive soul, my boy. Maybe she *was* a worthless human being, but she was still a human being."

He held up a finger.

"Not that on some level I don't think that she got what she deserved, but . . . my God, how horrible."

"It was," Harry agreed.

"You don't know the half of it. That book must have weighed a ton."

Jackson stood up.

"Get me another drink, would you? I don't want to risk breaking my neck in this place."

Jackson sat back down.

"Why am I living like this?" he asked himself. "Why?"

Harry found some Scotch, watered it down significantly and brought it to him.

"Jackson, I need you to tell me something," Harry said. "I think that people might be in danger."

"People *are* in danger," Jackson said. "*I* am in danger." He spoke with that sudden menacing clarity that drunks can have.

"Why, Jackson?"

Jackson looked out the window past a bulge in the drapes that I thought was Marlin. Once again there would be no getting near him. I could only hope that the Guatemalan tree sloth was unharmed.

Jackson reached out and grabbed Harry's arm and squeezed. When he released his grip, my owner's arm bore the angry impressions of Jackson's fingers.

"Harry, this is the most serious problem I have ever had in my life. The most serious," Jackson emphasized. "It was bad yesterday before Beatrice died. It's worse today. I'm trapped."

"Trapped?"

"Bad things happened. Bad things are about to happen. But my hands are too dirty to do anything about it."

"Tell me what you were going to tell me

yesterday."

"Yesterday?"

"Before the phone rang. Before we went to Lavery's. Tell me about how you think Beatrice killed Overton."

"It's not *think* anymore, Harry — it's *thought.* I was wrong. Beatrice didn't kill anyone. The person who killed Beatrice is the same person who killed Overton. And that person is Michael."

"I don't understand."

"Harry, I have done something so stupid . . . so stupid . . . And now — for all intents and purposes — I am an accomplice in Overton's death. I didn't realize the consequences at the time. I was only thinking of her good. Her good, goddamn it. It was so hard to believe that he had been murdered at all. That kind of thing just doesn't happen in real life. I mean, does it? Of course not. At least that kind of thing has never happened in my life. Plenty of men drop dead of a heart attack. Plenty. Leading cause of death . . ." Jackson threatened to ramble on.

"Who's 'her'?" asked Harry.

"She contacted me."

"Who?"

"Iris."

"I thought Iris never contacted you?"

"Ay, there's the rub."

"When?"

"Less than an hour after Overton died, I received a phone call from her. She said that the whole story was too complicated to relate. She said she was very afraid. Imagine how I felt. I hadn't heard her voice in almost three decades. There she was on the phone and she needed me. *She* needed *me.* I asked her what she was afraid of. She told me that Overton had been murdered."

"Why didn't she tell the police?"

"They weren't involved at that point. As it turned out they never got involved. Now I can see it was stupid, but at the time I thought I was being noble. Iris needed me so much. When someone is scared, they wrap you up in their fear. I forgot I had options."

"What else did she say?"

"Iris was convinced that something in the bathroom had killed Overton. She said that if it was found by the authorities, she would be implicated in his death."

"That's sort of vague."

"It *was* vague but it was urgent."

Jackson sank even deeper into the sofa.

"You know, my father had a saying. He used to drive me crazy with it: 'Don't confuse what is merely urgent with what is truly important.' What Iris was talking about that night was merely urgent. Nothing had to be done right away. *Nothing.*"

"But you did something anyway?"

"Iris told me that there was a shopping bag in the bathroom. She said that something was in the bag, wrapped in cardboard. She refused to say what was in the bag. She said I shouldn't know — that I didn't need to know. She wanted me to get the bag out of the apartment and dispose of it somewhere."

Harry shook his head.

"That's no good, Jackson."

"She said she wouldn't be home when I got there. She asked if I still had the key to the apartment."

Jackson motioned to the wall by the front door. A key hung on a red ribbon next to a Celtic cross made of ceramic.

"It's been in that spot since I bought the place."

"So you went to the apartment and got rid of the thing?"

"She asked if I could get there no later than midnight. I said yes. She thanked me and hung up. She had left word with the doorman that I would be coming, and he let me go straight up. The apartment was dark. I searched for the lights but couldn't find them. I groped my way down the hallway to the bathroom. It was strange to be there again after so many years. The shopping bag was right against the wall where Iris said it would be. As I was about to leave, I heard the front door open. It was Beatrice. She asked me what I was doing. Before I could answer she told me to leave. Something about seeing her there made me so angry. The impudence of the woman, I thought, leaching off Iris and telling me — the actual owner of the apartment — to get out. This was too much. I have never been a violent man, but I grabbed her and pushed her up against some shelves. Iris hadn't given me any details of the events of that night, but I had some ideas of my own. I was convinced that Beatrice was somehow involved. I told her that if Iris was harmed in any way, she would answer for it."

Jackson smiled, a thin, self-conscious smile.

"It's funny what we resort to in extremis. I sounded like a thug from a B-movie. I actually told Beatrice that she was walking around with a target on her back. Ridiculous. But you have to understand how upset I was. Then I left the apartment."

"You got rid of whatever it was?"

"No," Jackson said. "It's right over there."

He pointed at a shopping bag that sat beside the yellow box of Cuban cigars on the end table.

"Bring it over here," Jackson instructed. Harry brought the bag over.

"It's incredibly heavy," Harry said.

Jackson reached down into the bag and with great effort placed a strange-looking object on his lap.

"What is it?" Harry asked.

"I have no idea but I think it had something to do with Overton's death."

Yours Truly could have shed light on the question for the pair. In fact, another *Eureka* was in order. The *MythBusters* had only momentarily flummoxed me. Now that I saw the device with its layers and layers of tightly coiled copper wire, everything fell into place. Jackson was holding a primitive but powerful electromagnet. Overton had not been electrocuted. Instead, he had walked into a much more nuanced murder — an enclosed and highly magnetized death chamber that caused his pacemaker to go haywire and consequently induced a fatal arrhythmia. Overton might have thought he had been electrocuted *(perhaps there was some electricity running through that toilet after all);* but (Elektra) magnetism was to blame.

Jackson Wrestles
with Love
A Favor is Required

I emerged from my triumphant mental victory lap as Jackson continued to drunkenly relate his account to Harry.

"A few days later, I got another call from Iris. I told her that I had gotten rid of the bag and she thanked me. She mentioned that Overton's autopsy had shown no foul play — and suggested that nothing had happened after all. She said that maybe she had a case of nerves. I asked what would have made her get so carried away. She told me that it was Beatrice — that Beatrice had somehow involved her in a convoluted scheme to get Overton to commit to her. The plan was to use some sort of séance: Beatrice to play the psychic and deliver convenient instructions from the person of Overton's first wife."

"Madame Sosostris was Beatrice?" Harry asked. "That explains why she seemed so familiar to me."

"Is that what she called herself?" Jackson laughed. "That woman was many things but dull wasn't one of them."

Jackson tapped his empty glass and Harry refilled it with more watered-down Scotch.

"Beatrice was going to have Overton's dead wife encourage him to marry Iris. Give him the okay, so to speak. But before the séance began, Beatrice told her that the plan was more complicated. She told her that something unpleasant was going to happen to Overton that would make him more suggestible."

Jackson emptied his glass.

"You're right, Harry. If Iris had only gone to the police, the whole thing could have been resolved."

"Couldn't it now?" Harry asked.

"I don't think so. Chivalry might be dead, Harry, but God knows I have spent my life ready to put my cape over any mud puddles that that woman might come across and I won't stop now. Every possibility threatens Iris. I've lived a kind of half-life because of her and when you've done something for so long, things that seemed horrific, impossible, well off the scale when you were young — being an accomplice in a murder, for example — begin to seem almost reasonable, even acceptable, in relation to other concerns."

"Jackson, won't it only get worse? I mean Beatrice is dead now. The police are going to backtrack to Overton. They'll make connections."

"Maybe."

"You could get into trouble."

"I'm not worried about myself, Harry."

"You should be."

Jackson sighed. "Harry, I need you. Help me protect Iris."

"How can I do that, Jackson?"

"If there is something that will show that Michael is responsible, Iris will be safe."

"I'm no detective," Harry objected. "And besides what if Michael isn't responsible?"

"Nonsense. I'm sure Michael's the one and that's the problem with you young people today — you're overspecialized. You don't think you're capable of doing anything outside your narrow field. I'm talking about common sense and observation. Besides your fingerprints are on that shopping bag now."

Harry rose abruptly from his chair.

"Don't listen to me, Harry," Jackson said. "That was low and I'm a fool. I'm also very drunk."

"You are drunk," Harry agreed. "But you're a good man, Jackson."

A Killer is
Revealed
A Beret is
Returned

A short time later Jackson fell into a Scotch-induced slumber. Harry pulled a blanket out from beneath the massive *Oxford English Dictionary* and tucked it around him. Then we left.

"What are we going to do, Randolph?" Harry asked.

We had turned onto Central Park West and were headed home.

I have always been fascinated by the concept of evil. Psychiatrists who specialize in the criminal mind have tended to avoid the term when describing those they analyze because its cultural potency overshadows other clinical possibilities like depression, narcissism, et cetera.

Recently, however, a handful of psychiatrists have embraced the notion that there is no better word than *evil* for describing the kind of people behind acts of depravity and slaughter in which the killer not only lacks remorse but cannot see the wrong in what he or she has done.

These people not only fail to see the wrong, they often enjoy the pain and terror they cause. Some do so while seeming to be creatures of the most refined tastes and sensitive natures. Doing evil is one thing; being evil quite another.

Jackson and Michael were guilty of nothing more than being fools for Iris. Iris was not only traffic control for acquiring and disposing of the means of Overton's death; she was the cause of all the traffic. Marlin had seen Michael bring the electromagnet and possibly install it under Iris's gaze a few days before Overton's death. Jackson had removed the electromagnet at Iris's request.

I reflected on Iris's scent.

So many words and phrases that are part of human language make better sense when you understand the world through the nose of a dog. A dog, as I've mentioned, really is able to *smell* trouble. Corruption often *reeks*, usually with an odor like bad oysters. But murderous psychopaths — those smooth and inscrutable machines — have the most terrifying smell of all: the smell of absence. Their scent is the olfactory equivalent of the forsaken shades Dante found in his *Inferno,* eternally drifting shells, anonymous, incapable of remorse, damned. I had smelled my first psychopath in Iris.

My mind returned to the afternoon we spent at Iris's apartment and that indefinite smell. It skipped ahead to Beatrice lying beneath the Audubon volume. The same smell was there. This was Iris's smell, unique in its blankness, its nothingness.

Iris had been so difficult for me to read because there was nothing there to read. She had no moods. She couldn't get offended. She couldn't get upset or angry or hurt or joyful. There was never a specific emotion, only the lack of one. Iris was no one, not even herself. She had no moral anchor. She had no fear. She possessed the perfect innocence of a child pulling the wings off a fly. She was nothing, and as a result she was capable of anything.

When we arrived home, I made a beeline for the kitchen table so that Harry would be reminded about the latest message and recognize that Iris was guilty.

"What's going on, boy?" Harry asked.

I intensely dislike being called *boy,* but overlooked the term for the greater good.

Harry saw the message and sat down in front of it. He began to drum his fingers.

Unfortunately, he did not immediately come to the correct conclusion.

"It could be Iris, but it could also be Michael."

Harry shook his head.

"It says don't be afraid of Michael."

He tapped his fingers.

"But it doesn't say that Michael isn't the one."

He shook his head again.

"It could be Michael, but it could also be Iris."

I barked.

"It's Michael," Harry said, rapidly going in the wrong direction.

There are times in life when one has to jump from the trapeze one is holding to the trapeze that has not yet arrived. Reflection and inaction create a false world built on distorted measures of possibility and hindsight. One must risk. The sidelines are the small town of the soul.

"It *is* Michael," Harry insisted.

There was no way for me to correct my owner's mistake with my body's limited ability to express itself. The trapeze was slipping backward away from the truth and to slip away from the truth was to allow the possibility of more death. So I let go of the trapeze.

I put my front paws on Harry's lap and propped myself up at the table to begin the laborious job of rearranging letters with my nose. When Harry understood what I was doing, a silence overwhelmed the room. It was the profound stillness of my owner's awe.

"Amazing," he gasped.

Ten minutes must have passed as I re-shuffled letters into a brief command:

IRIS KILLER
DEVICE AN ELECTROMAGNET
INTERRUPTED OVERTON PACEMAKER
SAVE JACKSON AND MICHAEL

I dropped back down to the floor.

"Amazing."

Now I had really done it. I had altered our relationship forever. He would understand that I was fully cognizant. The consequences were grave and unknowable.

Thankfully, Harry brought us back from this abyss with his appalling habit of misinterpreting the obvious through the far-fetched lens of the supernatural.

"You *are* inspired, aren't you, boy? I've never heard of the spirit world working so directly through animal mediums before — but why not use a simple dog as a conduit for profound truths?"

Before my owner could continue in this vein, there was a knock on the door. It was Lieutenant Peter T. Davis of the New York City Police Department.

"Happy New Year, Harry," Lieutenant Davis said.

"Happy New Year, Lieutenant."

Lieutenant Davis had overseen the investigation into Imogen's disappearance and developed a kind of friendship with my owner. He possessed a gentle, reflective demeanor that suggested a life of contemplation and spiritual seeking — a quality quite surprising in a police detective. Indeed, in his former life he had been a Buddhist monk, spending more than a decade high in the mountains of Nepal.

"I can't stay for long, Harry, but I brought this," he said.

Lieutenant Davis held out a clear plastic bag.

"The beret," Harry said softly, weighing it in one hand.

The lieutenant nodded.

"The department released it today and I thought you might want it . . . It's been a year."

"A year," Harry echoed.

Today was the anniversary of the day our

mistress went to get bread and didn't come home.

"I'm sorry, Harry," Lieutenant Davis said.

The detective scanned the apartment.

"Peter, if there was trouble — something I had to talk to you about? Not as a friend, but as a detective," Harry said.

"What's going on?" Lieutenant Davis asked.

"It's not about Imogen."

The lieutenant's eyes fell on the kitchen table.

"You like cereal?"

"It's been a hard couple of weeks," my owner said.

"You know I lost my wife five years ago."

Harry nodded.

"You never get over it, but sooner or later it gets over you."

"But it's not about Imogen."

"You certain about that?"

"And it's not about me exactly."

"A friend?"

"A friend."

Harry rubbed his forehead with the base of his palm.

"I don't know how it's going to develop, but I might need to contact you very soon."

"Harry, I have no idea what you're talking about."

"Maybe it's better that way."

"Probably not."

"I shouldn't have mentioned it."

"You have my cell phone number?"

"Yeah."

"My pager?"

"Yeah."

"My home number?"

"I've got them all."

"Use them."

Harry nodded.

"It's going to be okay, Harry," the lieutenant said. "Don't get too worked up about other stuff. Every year to the day after I lost Nancy — maybe for the first three — I would have a panic. Sweats, jitters, that sort of thing. I finally saw someone about it. You know what they call it? Anniversary syndrome. Sometimes you might even forget but it's in your bones somewhere. Your bones remember. It's a deep thing . . . losing."

"Thanks, Peter."

"Do you want the *Post?*" the lieutenant asked.

He handed my owner the tabloid.

Peter left and Harry threw the newspaper front page up into my corner without looking at the headline. He flopped into the La-Z-Boy and turned on the television. Zest

Kilpatrick, wearing a bright green top with a carnation in her hair, was outlining an antistress checklist for those who might be suffering from the post-holiday blues.

(1) Take ten minutes with your family to talk about the day's events, (2) have a special meal time and stick to it; (3) remember, eat slowly; (4) watch your consumption of alcohol and caffeine; and — last but not least — (5) stay away from anxiety-inducing people.

"I'll start with you," Harry muttered and switched off the television. Then he lay back with the beret on his chest and closed his eyes.

Harry Solves a Puzzle
A Dog Races into Danger on a Still-Empty Stomach

Harry did not rest for long. Five minutes after he had closed his eyes, the phone rang. Harry let the machine pick up. He shouldn't have. It was Michael and the message was urgent.

"Harry, I have to meet you. I am at Iris's apartment. I have some photos you need to see." There was a pause and then a frantic, "She's here."

Harry fumbled for the phone, but the line was dead. He grabbed his jacket and we were about to head out the door when something on the kitchen table caught his eye and he stopped. He began pushing letters around with his fingers.

"Cymbeline." Harry read. "That was the play I waited for hours to get tickets for Imogen . . . strange."

I could not resist the temptation to see

what had made Harry say this and climbed up onto the chair beside him. What I saw stunned me. My owner had solved in an instant the code that I had virtually given up on. He had moved every other letter half an inch or so down — enough for the word *Cymbeline* to appear out of the original string of letters. The code had not been sophisticated at all. It was a simple extra-letter cipher. Extraneous letters were added to pad the message and each of these was one letter higher in the alphabet than the letter that preceded it. Thus, *CDYZMNBCE-FLMIJNOEF* became *Cymbeline*. But why would Imogen have gone to so much trouble to deliver the name of a Shakespearean play? And just as I asked myself this question, I also knew the answer.

Cymbeline was the play from which her name was derived. But it was just one element of the plot of that play which really mattered. The character of Imogen is a princess who plays dead to protect herself and those she loves from the malevolent schemes of others. Imogen had encoded the play's name to make sure that we would understand how important this fact was to her disappearance. Our mistress had vanished to save us.

Harry attached my leash. Soon we were

out the door and for the second time that day my owner and I raced down Central Park West toward Jackson's street. Harry kept us at a jog as we passed under the long scaffold loggias that seem to be a permanent fixture of the grand residential buildings that line the avenue. My lungs were burning. My paws stung from an encounter with rock salt left over from the last snow.

And then I smelled it. We were almost there, but despite the better angels of my nature I came to a complete stop, jerking the leash with such force that it nearly dislocated my owner's shoulder.

"Randolph?" Harry asked. "What is it?"

"It" was the most sublime — and the most ill-timed — sidewalk paté I had ever encountered — a pile of inscrutable decay heaped a few inches from the curb. My senses were overcome, my nerves tingled with transcendent possibility, spirit and flesh soared with the promise of union and fulfillment. All commitments to Harry, Jackson and Imogen were momentarily vanquished.

How could a quick roll hurt?

I fought back with diminishing reason.

Every second counts. We must not stop.

Alas, reason and my purer intentions were powerless before the deep magic of sidewalk paté. I began to roll. And roll. And roll. The world around me dimmed as a profound bliss atomized my concentration. Somewhere in the distance, a female passerby observed:

"Aren't dogs funny?"

Then there was a firm yank on my collar. Like the dreaming character aloft in the clouds in *8 1/2,* Fellini's classic movie of anxiety and escape, I was dragged back down to earth.

I got to my feet and took one last fond look at the pile. I doubted that I would see its like again. We were on our way. This time Harry doubled the pace. We stood in the lobby of Iris's building a few minutes later — my owner barely out of breath; his pet risking cardiac arrest.

As I struggled to recover, Harry looked for the doorman, but there was no sign of him.

"Weird," Harry said.

He led me into the elevator and we rose slowly to the murderer's floor uncertain what we would find there. The elevator bell rang as usual when we arrived. But before Harry knocked on Iris's door, we took a moment to listen.

A Dog on His Own
A Lady Sing the Blues

The sounds from behind the door were not promising. Nor was the dominant smell: human terror, which I can best describe as a mixture of licorice and blood. There seemed to be three people inside the apartment: Iris, Jackson and Michael. Iris and Jackson were speaking. Michael was in the background. At first, he was moaning and then he seemed to be begging for help.

Harry motioned for me to stay put and disappeared into the elevator. I hoped he wasn't planning anything rash. I assumed the canine position of attentive seatedness, waiting, with increased heart rate, for what would come next.

Michael fell silent and footsteps approached the front door. I found myself staring up into Iris's face.

"That elevator bell is the most helpful early warning system," Iris said. "You're that boy's dog, aren't you? That handsome boy who believes in ghosts?"

She glanced up and down the corridor, took my leash and led me into the apartment. I offered no resistance.

"My God, you stink," Iris said, referring to the still exquisite odors emanating from my sidewalk paté–bedewed coat.

"Randolph, what are *you* doing here?" Jackson exclaimed.

He was tied up in a club chair on the opposite side of the room.

"Rotten timing, pup," he observed.

I followed Jackson's gaze. Michael's body was slumped over the dining room table. His head formed the center of a pool of blood — a piece of metal sunk deep into the base of his skull.

"Miss Scarlett with the candlestick in the living room slash dining room." Iris smiled.

Jackson's lifelong love had a pistol tucked into the belt of her white bathrobe and fresh blood on her hands.

"This is awful," Jackson muttered. "Awful, awful, awful."

Iris went to the windowsill and sat down. She held a cigarette and a sheaf of photographs that she had taken from the dead man. She began to flip through them.

"What a naughty little worm you were," Iris addressed Michael's body.

She held one photo up to Jackson. The photo showed the electromagnet propped against the bathroom wall.

"Evidence dispensed with," Iris said, tearing up the photograph and flipping its pieces out the window.

"Iris, please. You need help," Jackson implored.

"And look at this one. He found *this* one when he developed all the pictures in my camera," Iris said. She did not show the photo to Jackson, but I saw it clearly. It was a photo of Imogen.

"You *must* get help," Jackson insisted.

Iris tore the rest of the photographs up and threw them out the window. The pieces hung in space before being whisked away by a stiff wind like flakes in a storm.

"Aren't you sweet?" Iris said. "You still care for me after it would be obvious to anyone else that I am a monster."

"You're not a monster."

"What kind of man would hold on to someone who didn't give a damn about him?" Iris mused. "How many years has it been? Four decades."

Iris ashed her cigarette on the floor. "You're so pathetic."

"It's love," Jackson said. "You know love."

"I've never loved anyone. I'm not capable of it."

"You loved Overton."

"No, I didn't. People see what they want to see. Overton fit. Beatrice fit. Michael fit. You fit. People fit for a while and then they don't fit anymore."

"You're not yourself."

"I have never been more myself."

Jackson had sobered up since the morning. He looked at Iris as if she were on fire.

"Where can any of this get you?" Jackson asked.

"Does it matter?"

Her smell was even more indistinct than before if that was possible.

"But I protected you."

"If I had let you see me over the past three decades, you wouldn't have," Iris said. "But I didn't."

She lit another cigarette.

"Do you remember Ann Jacobs?"

"Your roomate in college?"

"The very girl. How did she die?"

"Car accident."

"Ann was my first one," Iris said. "And Max Miller?"

"Ruptured appendix."

"Was it? And Richard Snow?"

"He drowned."

"Did he?"

Jackson dropped his head and closed his eyes.

"I don't know how I couldn't have known," he moaned.

"I didn't want you to know," Iris said.

"You're so unwell."

"How could I be unwell if I've never been any other way?"

"Why did you kill Overton?" Jackson asked.

"He wanted to write a book about my lethal proclivities and my family's fortune," Iris said. "That wasn't so bad in itself. It would have made a terrific read. But then I learned that he intended to bring my daughter into the story and that was unacceptable."

"Daughter?" Jackson asked. "I didn't know that you had a daughter."

Iris remained silent.

"And Michael? And Beatrice?" Jackson continued.

"To tie up loose ends," Iris said. "It will be the same with you. Beatrice had to die because she made the mistake of blackmailing me. Not only had the clever thing learned some of the unsavories in my past but she was also witness to the Overton séance adventure. Michael had to die because he was putting the pieces together about Overton's death, and then he made the mistake of following me to that apartment where Beatrice found herself buried in a book."

This explained why Michael had been able to pursue Harry and me into Central Park the day Beatrice died. He had followed Iris to Lavery's apartment first and then seen us leave.

At that moment, the door flew open. Harry burst into the room. I had hoped that my owner had gone for the authorities — apparently he had not, opting instead to retrieve the red-ribboned key from Jackson's apartment and attempt the adventure himself. Iris pointed the gun at Harry's stomach and he froze.

"Come in quietly and close the door," Iris said. "I have been waiting for you."

Harry did as he was told.

"Sit cross-legged on the floor exactly where you are."

My owner sat down on the floor and crossed his legs.

"Why didn't I hear the elevator bell?" Iris asked.

"I took the stairs," Harry said.

She gestured at Michael's body. "Everything's gone to pot," Iris observed. "This will be a challenge to clean up."

Then when things looked most bleak, Harry impressed me with his calm.

"I know how you killed Overton," my owner said with a firmness that had been missing from his voice for many months. "You used an electromagnet and it disrupted his pacemaker."

Iris raised her eyebrows. She wandered over to Michael and contemplated his wound. Then she began to trace something in the blood on the table with the barrel of her gun.

"I could tell *you* a thing or two of interest as well," she said.

"You could?" Harry asked.

"You had a lady love. Went for bread and did not return. By the name of Imogen."

"What do you know?"

"She wore a red beret," Iris said. "One would have to travel very far afield to learn all of the story, but you have caught me at a talkative moment. Haven't you wondered why you were invited to the séance the night Overton died?"

"Not really," Harry said.

"I sent you the invitation," Iris said. "I got your address through Overton. He got your address through dear Imogen herself. I wanted you to come."

"Why?"

"I wanted to meet the man my daughter loved," Iris said.

"You're her . . ." Harry was dumbfounded.

"That's right. You can say it: I'm her mother," Iris said.

"But Imogen's parents were killed when she was a baby," Harry insisted.

"Metaphorically speaking they were killed perhaps. I only met the girl once, and as an adult. A beautiful girl. You see, Overton found her for me. He might have been a hack but he was a superb reporter. He managed to do something I had never been able to do — he tracked her down. They tried to keep me from her. I mean they tried to keep *her* from me. They thought I'd use her to get at it."

"What's 'it'?"

"The fortune. You see we — she and I — are the beneficiaries of one of the greatest uranium discoveries of the twentieth century. My grandfather, Imogen's great-grandfather, found a ridge in the middle of the Australian Outback a hundred feet high, a hundred yards wide and fifty miles long. Filled with uranium. They mined it for fifty years and only scratched that ridge. I was meant to inherit it, but my father was wise to who I was — he made certain that the fortune went around me. He wasn't too sure how my daughter was going to turn out either, even after they took her away from me, so everything is in a trust and she will only inherit it if she successfully turns thirty. And by successfully, I mean, if she doesn't go mad or turn out to be a psychopath like her mother."

"This is crazy," Harry said.

"Don't believe me, then. It doesn't matter. Imogen is gone. Perhaps she is gone for good. But she knew. She believed me when I told her."

Iris lapsed into silence.

"You saw her?" Harry stammered. "Before she disappeared?"

"The very day," Iris said. "I daresay I was the cause."

"That means she's alive," Harry said.

"I'm surprised he hasn't visited you yet," Iris said, ignoring Harry's statement.

"Who?" Harry asked.

"The guardian of the fortune — a cattleman and a lawyer. He was my father's fast friend," Iris said. "He's an enormous man and he favors those wide-brimmed Australian hats. The Akubra hats. An outback character like that is sure to stand out on the streets of New York."

"What's his name?"

"I've told you enough," Iris said. "You haven't seen him, have you?"

Harry shook his head.

"He's a watcher that one. Very patient. I'm sure he's out there somewhere," Iris said.

Harry might not have seen this man, but his dog felt certain that he had. Iris's Australian guardian of the fortune sounded very much like the menacing figure we almost encountered on Christmas night.

"Imogen's alive," Harry whispered.

"Oh, I wouldn't be too sure about that," Iris said. "Maybe something that I said made her disappear. Maybe I killed her. I'll never tell."

"What do you know?" Harry insisted. But Iris had slipped away from direct statements and clear answers and spoke now with the prophetic vagueness of a fortune-teller.

"I know that there are tragedies and there are comedies," she said. "I know that there are comedies that look like tragedies. I know that sometimes the living appear dead and the dead appear to be living. There is a time to reconsider everything that has been assumed and believed to be true. Unfortunately, you won't have much time to reconsider anything."

"What more do you know about Imogen?"

Harry demanded.

Iris said nothing.

"The police are on their way," Harry said. "They know what you did."

She went to the kitchen and put a mug of water with a tea bag in the microwave. Then she set the timer for one minute.

"Decisions must be made then," Iris said.

She returned to the open window.

"Let's have some music."

She pushed a button on the stereo's remote control. Billie Holiday sang about lost love. Iris took the gun out of her bathrobe and raised it to Jackson's head. The day was already well advanced and the late afternoon sun reflected off the windows of the building opposite.

"I have been bored so long that today I think I'm going to do something different," Iris said.

A gust of air passed through the open window and mussed her hair. Jackson's head remained slumped. He did not look up.

Billie went into the refrain. Her voice stretched to a tormented breaking:

Love me or leave me.

A shot rang out. My sensitive ears shattered and I felt momentarily dizzy. Iris stumbled backward against the windowsill and dropped the gun.

"What did you mean about the red beret?" Harry asked. He held a pistol. It was Grandfather Oswald's Colt .45 service revolver from World War II.

"Socrates drank hemlock," Iris said weakly. "Mithridates fell on his sword."

Billie continued to sing about choosing loneliness over happiness.

"I never liked the Blues," Iris said. "Now I know why."

She slid backward off the windowsill and out into space with the same disinterest that someone might brush a bit of lint off a jacket.

EPILOGUE

In the immediate aftermath of Iris's death, Imogen's trail went cold. Jackson was soon cleared of any wrongdoing and spent a great deal of time holed up in his suite recuperating from his disillusionment and brush with death in the company of a much-relieved Guatemalan tree sloth. Harry was cleared of any charges because his handgun was properly registered and the shooting was obviously in self-defense. The police, led by Lieutenant Davis, seemed fascinated by the contraption responsible for Overton's death but since the murderer, Iris, and her possible coconspirators and victims Michael and Beatrice, were dead, no further investigation was planned. No traces of the photographs were found, but I surmised that Michael had likely taken the pictures of the electromagnet with the camera that already had been used by Iris to take photos of Imogen. Thus, when Michael had the roll of film developed, these pictures were also developed. Where the negatives might be remained a mystery as did so many things.

How much of what Iris said before she died was true? Would the menacing figure, the guardian she talked about, materialize? Would Imogen? What should Harry and I do next?

A few weeks later at twilight, we were walking back home through Central Park after a wander through the Ramble. My owner and I had found a new spot for our walks. Both of us were tired of the Bull Moose Dog Run — too many complications and too many memories. There had been another big snow, but we were in the middle of a midwinter thaw. The few inches of snow covering the ground had melted quickly as the temperature climbed well above freezing.

We trudged up a hill to the exit. An old woman approached us before we reached Eighty-sixth street. She looked like one's mental image of an ancient prophetess.

She paused before us in the dim light. I could barely see her lips move as she spoke.

"There's life under this snow," she whispered.

She moved on and disappeared into a darkening clutch of trees.

It was a strange moment, heavy with possibility. With the melting snow, the human condition is revealed, especially in Manhattan. Things that were thrown away when people thought the weather would cover them up slowly begin to reemerge. The number of dog "surprises" increases exponentially. There was much waiting beneath the snow, archeological layers of laziness, disregard and negligence.

This was one kind of life, but there was also the other life: the cycle of regeneration. Worms had already begun to do their work of enriching the soil. Roots pushed blindly away in response to the approaching vernal equinox. Life was relentless. It pushed even the most resistant beings forward with its seasonal demands.

Harry and I had just crossed Central Park West and were walking up toward the Eighty-eighth Street entrance to the C and B trains when I suddenly smelled Imogen. This scent was *hers.* There could be no mistake. The closest parallel is a mix of sandalwood, pear and cotton. Imogen was alive.

Objects were blurry in the failing light. People were all about, blocking my view with a thicket of legs.

Then I saw her. She was dressed in a dark

coat. Her hair had been cropped so short that her appearance was radically altered and she wore high heels, something she had rarely done. But I knew my mistress.

She had reached the subway entrance and was descending underground. I wrenched myself free of Harry and raced after her. When I arrived at the top of the stairs, Imogen was already at the bottom. She held her MetroCard in her right hand. I knew the turnstiles were only a few paces from her. I jumped down the stairs, hitting the midway point with a thud and feeling the rest of my bulk push forward painfully into my chest. But I got to my feet and jumped again. As I recovered, I heard the swipe of Imogen's MetroCard and the clank of the turnstile swinging her onto the subway platform just as an uptown train arrived.

There was nothing I could do but watch and bark.

Imogen didn't turn around. The train came to a halt, its doors slid open, she boarded and disappeared from sight. The doors slid shut and the train began to move, gradually gaining speed until it vanished into the tunnel with a metallic wail.

I hadn't seen her face, but her smell clung to my nose. There was fear in that scent and deceit and a mother lode of sadness.

Harry reached me.

"Don't you *ever* run off like that again," Harry said.

Then he stooped down, lifted me off my paws and carried me homeward up the stairs.

ABOUT THE AUTHOR

J. F. Englert, a writer of fiction and nonfiction for both book and screen, lives in Manhattan with his wife, P. Englert, daughter, C. Englert, and dog, R. Englert.

The employees of Thorndike Press hope you have enjoyed this Large Print book. All our Thorndike and Wheeler Large Print titles are designed for easy reading, and all our books are made to last. Other Thorndike Press Large Print books are available at your library, through selected bookstores, or directly from us.

For information about titles, please call:
(800) 223-1244

or visit our Web site at:
www.gale.com/thorndike
www.gale.com/wheeler

To share your comments, please write:
Publisher
Thorndike Press
295 Kennedy Memorial Drive
Waterville, ME 04901